Perfect FORMATION

KB Alan

ELLORA'S CAVE
ROMANTICA PUBLISHING

An Ellora's Cave Romantica Publication

www.ellorascave.com

Perfect Formation

ISBN 9781419961878
ALL RIGHTS RESERVED.
Perfect Formation Copyright © 2009 KB Alan
Edited by Sue-Ellen Gower.
Cover art by Syneca.

Electronic book publication March 2009
Trade paperback publication 2010

PERFECT FORMATION

ह०

Trademarks Acknowledgement

ℰℴ

Chapter One

ဘာ

Caleb Black checked his watch as he exited his SUV. It was almost one o'clock in the morning. His destination was a lively Irish bar on the main street of town, owned by his brother Sean. He had been working later than expected but Sean and his wife Lisa were closing tonight, so the late hour shouldn't be a problem.

Up ahead, the door of the bar, *Roisin Dubh*, swung open, emitting a man and a woman clinging to each other, clearly drunk. The woman's laugh captured Caleb's attention. Her long, thick hair was rich brown and his fingers itched to run through it. The man's hand on her ass showed off her sexy curves to great appeal. For that matter, there wasn't anything wrong with the man's ass, either.

They stopped under a streetlight at the curb in front of the bar, hanging on to each other. Caleb chuckled as a wayward curl defied the man's clumsy attempt to push it back and it flopped onto his forehead, the muted light picking up golden highlights in the light brown locks. His eyes tracked down over strong features to full lips that invited a nibble or two.

Caleb suppressed a slight groan as the woman brought one hand up to the man's neck and rested her head on his shoulder. He wanted to feel that slight weight on his own shoulder. Well, on his chest anyway, she wouldn't have been able to reach his shoulder. Something about the two of them together hit all of his buttons just right. He tried to determine which he found more attractive as he began walking again, heading toward the pub door.

The man started to fall, obviously trying to let go of the woman so as not to drag her down with him. She was just as

7

obviously trying to hold him up, and not about to let go. Caleb hurried to reach them and held the man steady while he got his feet back under him.

Bracing one hand on Caleb's shoulder, the man closed his eyes in an obvious attempt to gain his equilibrium.

"Thanks."

Caleb looked at the woman who was eyeing him like a box of chocolates.

"Yummmmm," she murmured under her breath, though Caleb heard it clearly. She put one hand out and laid it on his chest, her eyes glassy, her expression dreamy. She gave a tiny whimper and her fingers gripped tightly into him. Caleb worked hard not to smile. He checked her companion for a reaction, but the man's eyes were still closed.

"Taryn," the man said, then went quiet.

"Richard," Taryn answered.

"Taryn," Richard tried again. "Are we still moving?"

Taryn seemed to think this over for a minute, but then lost track of the question.

"Ricky, he's so frickin' *hot*," she said, somehow under the illusion that Caleb couldn't hear her. Her eyes hadn't left his chest, but now they began to make their way south.

Richard blinked his eyes open, looked at Taryn, then followed her gaze straight to Caleb's crotch. He licked his lips. His hand clenched where it rested on Caleb's shoulder as he swayed.

"Taryn."

"Richard."

"Taryn, you are really drunk."

"Okay."

"No, I mean really. Are you aware that you're staring at this nice man's crotch?"

Taryn considered this. "Yes, but I don't think it's real."

Caleb gave an astonished gasp, while Richard blinked some more. "It looks real to me. It looks real big. It looks real..." He licked his lips again, swallowed hard.

Taryn's brows crinkled in confusion. "No, I mean, I don't think the man is real. This is a dream, or maybe an hallucination. He's like, our dream man or something, don't you think? What're the chances a perfect man would be standing right here, right now, while we're really drunk?" she asked.

Richard started to nod his head and then started to fall over. Caleb stepped in closer to prop him up, bringing the three of them into a tight formation. He couldn't remember the last time he had been so entertained by such nonsense. Drunk people tended to strike him as very stupid, but he liked these two. And not because they were attractive, but because they seemed like nice people. He snorted his disbelief at himself. His movement closer to the girl had gotten her hand moving and it began to roam his chest.

"Well," Richard said. "Is it your dream, or my dream?"

This stumped Taryn for a good minute.

"Maybe it's my dream," Caleb threw in.

Taryn's hand on his chest tightened and Richard's moved down from his shoulder to his biceps.

"Huh," they both said, then looked at each other.

"Do you know this hot man, and you've been holding out on me? Is he gay?" Taryn asked Richard.

"No. Do you know him and you've been holding out on me, worried he'd turn gay if he met me?" Richard asked in return.

"No," Taryn said, then turned back to Caleb. "It can't be your dream, you don't know us."

"I'm Caleb," he said.

"Oh," Taryn said.

"Huh," Richard said.

"This must be your dream," said Taryn. "If it was my dream I'd be naked by now."

"You don't think we'd be naked by now if this was my dream?"

"Oh. Maybe it is my dream, 'cause if it was your dream, I don't think I'd be here right now. You don't dream about me with other men, do you?"

"I never have before, but it seems like a fine time to start."

"Do you dream about Richard with other men?" Caleb asked Taryn.

"Well, I had that weird dream where he was being stalked by that creepy doctor guy on that show *Doctor England, MD*. Remember that, Richard?"

"No," Richard said. "I don't think I was there for that dream."

"And then there was the dream with that hunky action hero, from that movie this summer, remember, Ricky?" Taryn went on, not listening. Her eyes got wide and dreamy. "That was an *excellent* dream. You were still seeing Bruce then, so I might not have told you about that one. I was getting horny, because we hadn't had sex in like, six months. I had to go buy a new vibrator after that dream." She closed her eyes, smiling as she remembered.

"Huh," Richard said. "I can't believe you didn't tell me about that one. Taryn."

"Ricky."

"I don't think we're dreaming."

There was silence for a few minutes.

"I don't ever remember dreaming that I was going to throw up before."

"Maybe you guys should walk down to the diner on the corner. Get some food into you," Caleb suggested.

"How long have we been out here?" Taryn asked. "The taxi still hasn't shown up." She looked up and down the street in irritation.

"About fifteen minutes," Caleb told her. "You should get some food into your systems, soak up some of the alcohol."

Taryn looked at him some more, blinked a few times. Then the color washed out of her face. "Oh shit. I'm not dreaming, am I?"

"Nope. Neither am I. Neither is Richard."

She blushed. "I'm sorry, I don't usually drink this much. I'm sorry we're acting like idiots. You don't have to stand here. We can wait for the taxi." Her eyes were fixed on his chest, but not quite in the awe-inspired way as before.

"Don't worry about it."

Richard spoke up. "I think the food thing is a good idea, Tare. We should have thought of it. We'll go down to the diner. By the time we sober up a bit, maybe we'll have managed to forget that we're idiots."

"You guys don't do this kind of thing much, do you?" Caleb asked.

"Proposition studly strangers?" Richard asked.

"Caress strange men in public?" Taryn asked.

"Drink," Caleb answered.

"Caleb?"

"Yes?"

"I just wanted to say, before I get sober enough to care that I'm a fool, that I'm pretty sure I've soaked through my panties as well as my jeans, 'cause you guys are so fucking sexy. Thank you. Bye." With obvious care, she took her hands from both men, turned around and began walking toward the diner with only a slight wobble to her gait.

"Damn," Richard said.

"Damn," Caleb agreed.

Richard began to follow Taryn, and Caleb began to follow Richard. He pulled out his cell phone and sent a quick text message to his brother to let him know he wouldn't be in tonight.

Taryn feared she was sobering up. She was not completely sure, as she wasn't used to being drunk in the first place, but she was pretty certain that an hour ago she would have hardly remembered she'd said those words to Richard and a stranger, let alone be freaking out about them.

She walked into the diner and straight to a booth, sitting down with her back to the door, not wanting to see who might follow her inside. She managed a weak smile at the waitress who materialized and asked for a cherry Coke and a chocolate milkshake. Taryn put her elbows on the table and her head in her hands and stared down at the table.

She heard the two men slide into the seat across from her and managed, just barely, not to whimper. She was sure her face was still as red as the table, though. She heaved a huge sigh and sat back, her gaze straight ahead, right between the two men's faces. Richard ordered a strawberry shake and an iced tea, Caleb ordered black coffee, and the waitress left.

"Taryn."

A beat. Then two.

"Caleb."

"You're not allowed to say things like that then walk away."

"I'm not?" Her brow crinkled. "Says who?"

"Me."

"Huh." Taryn looked at Richard, raised her eyebrow at him.

Richard just shrugged his shoulders and mouthed, "Oh my *God.*" Or maybe it was "He's so *hot.*"

Either way, Taryn had to agree, so she nodded her head, looked at Caleb and said, "Sorry."

Caleb nodded in return.

"Caleb."

"Richard."

"What are you...I mean, why are you...I mean, who..." Richard stopped.

Caleb looked at Taryn for an interpretation.

"I'm just as confused as he is. We don't usually do strangers."

Caleb's eyebrows went up, Richard began to choke and Taryn's eyes went wide.

"That's not what I meant," she squeaked.

"So you do," Caleb purred at her, "do strangers?"

She whimpered.

"What she meant was, we're kind of shy and besides, we think most people are irritating, so we don't do so well at the whole 'meeting new people' thing."

Taryn nodded emphatically, giving Richard a grateful look.

The waitress brought their drinks. Caleb looked at them sternly and said, "Food."

They both ordered burgers and Caleb ordered a piece of cherry pie. The waitress left. Taryn tried to think of something to say that had nothing to do with sex or strangers. She tried to remember if she had *ever* been so instantly attracted to a man before. Maybe it was being drunk. Maybe she should try that more often. Of course, with her luck, not to mention family history, she would be an alcoholic before the year was out. Probably not worth it. She sucked on her milkshake, eyes staring down into the glass, while she considered what had happened since leaving the bar.

"Taryn."

She looked up at her best friend.

"He's still here."

Taryn glanced at Caleb then looked at Richard, confused. "Huh?"

"He hasn't called the funny farm to come take us away. Or the prude police to come lock us up."

Taryn considered this then looked back at Caleb. Almond-brown eyes watched her. The man was gorgeous— short, dark brown hair, his skin tan, different from Richard's natural olive, as if he spent a lot of time outside. Muscular, but not overly so. She couldn't get the phrase "tall, dark and handsome" out of her head. Her eyes began to glaze and she forgot what she'd been thinking about. The corner of his mouth quirked up as if he knew that.

"Ricky."

"Taryn."

She swallowed, caught in Caleb's gaze. "I love you." She couldn't decide what to make of the flicker in Caleb's face at that.

"I love you too. But?"

"But I'm about to melt into a puddle of goo, and he's just looking at me."

"I wish he'd look at m—" Richard's voice jerked into a squeak. Taryn looked at him and his eyes had gone wide. He flicked his eyes down to his leg, next to Caleb.

"I mean, yeah, me too."

Taryn nodded her head and decided she was done talking for a while. The waitress brought their burgers and Caleb's pie. Nobody spoke, they just ate.

Caleb pushed his pie plate away and wiped his lips with his napkin. Taryn's eyes remained riveted to his lips. He licked them then smiled just a bit when she gulped.

"Taryn. Richard."

"Caleb," they said at the same time.

"What's your story? You two are...?" He waved his hand between them. "A couple? Fuck buddies?"

Taryn looked at Richard and he nodded at her.

"We've been friends for a long time. After a few years, when we were both single, we started sleeping with each other. Sometimes one of us will meet someone we want to date, so we stop sleeping with each other. We've been doing that for about three years."

Caleb looked at Richard. "You usually sleep with women?"

"No, only one woman other than Taryn, and it didn't last very long."

Caleb looked at Taryn. "You usually sleep with men?"

"I've never slept with a woman."

"What about you?" Richard asked Caleb.

"I usually sleep with women," Caleb answered, looking Richard up and down. "But I've had my share of men."

"Together?" Taryn's voice cracked so she cleared her throat. "Do you ever sleep with them at the same time?"

"A couple of times," Caleb answered, "with two women. A couple of times with one woman, one other man."

"And how did you find that?" Richard asked.

"Each situation was different. There can be...some confusion about who's in charge."

Taryn's eyes went wide at this. She thought she might be bug-eyed at the end of this night. "In charge?"

Caleb's eyes pierced her. "That's right. What about you two—who's in charge when you're fucking?"

Taryn looked at Richard, who cleared his throat.

"I guess you could say we switch off." He flushed. Taryn wondered if he was flushing in manly embarrassment at not being in charge all of the time, or at the idea that Caleb would want to be. It was not something they had ever discussed, and

15

she realized he was right. Sometimes she was more aggressive, sometimes more nurturing, while other times he took charge, or was especially sweet and caring of her. They had a good, complementary relationship and suddenly she wondered if they were endangering that right now. If something happened with this man, even if it were only for one night, would it change them?

She finished her burger and soda and moved back to her milkshake.

Caleb's long right leg stretched out, coming to rest between her legs. Taryn was pretty sure the action was deliberate, but was becoming more and more sober, and less and less able to admit to how badly she wanted something to happen.

"Taryn."

"Caleb."

"Have you ever slept with a stranger?"

"No."

"Richard?"

"Not since college."

"Have you both been tested?"

Taryn's heart rate doubled. "Rick's a doctor, so he tests us every year, for everything, no matter what. I'm clean," she managed to get out.

"Ditto," Richard said, his voice thick. "And we made a promise not to have unprotected sex until we were married to someone else and knew we wouldn't be sleeping together anymore."

Caleb waited, then looked at them both sternly, until Richard said, "And you?"

"I haven't slept with a stranger in the last twelve years, and I get tested every year. I'm clean. I do not have unprotected sex, ever."

There was silence for a few minutes.

"Caleb." Taryn's voice was small.

"Taryn." Caleb's voice was gentle, soothing and in control.

"We're not…we don't…earlier we…" She gave up, took a long drink from her soda.

Caleb looked at Richard for an interpretation this time.

"She means that earlier, when we were so…um…outspoken, that's not what we're really like. If that's what you liked…" He stuttered to a stop, licked his lips.

"Why don't you guys worry about whether or not you want to see me again, and let me worry about what I want?"

They were silent again for a time.

"Caleb," Richard said.

"Yes?"

"Who are you?"

He seemed to think about the best way to answer that.

"You guys go to that pub much?"

"Sometimes we meet there after work, have a burger and a drink, listen to the music. We've never stayed that late before," Richard answered, pushing his plate away. The waitress came to take their plates and refill Caleb's coffee.

"Have you ever met the owner?"

"We met one of them, what was her name, Richard? Linda? No, Lisa. You were attracted to her, even before she got up and joined the band for a song."

Caleb nodded. "Lisa. She and her husband are the owners, and he's my brother, Sean." He looked at Richard. "You have excellent taste in women."

Taryn blushed.

"I grew up in the city, went into the military, retired, started a security firm, Precision Security, in Boston, with a partner. Moved here to North Fork last year when we decided a second, smaller office might be useful and I was getting tired of the city."

The waitress asked if they needed anything else and left the check when they declined. Caleb asked her for a pen.

Taryn was losing steam, fast, and could tell that Richard was as well. He'd had a long, tough day, which had led to her encouraging him to let loose tonight. She had a feeling Caleb had realized this before either of them.

He took a napkin from the dispenser and handed it and a pen to Taryn. She looked at him for a few seconds, then at Richard, then down at the napkin. She drew in a deep breath and wrote down her name and cell phone number. She slid it across the table to Caleb, not meeting his eyes. Caleb handed it to Richard. Richard wrote on it and gave it back to Caleb.

He looked down at the napkin. "Taryn Moss. Richard Daniels." He looked back up at them. "I'm Caleb Black. It's been my pleasure to meet you both tonight. I hope you'll have dinner with me sometime this week. I'll call you, see if we can set something up." He stood up, pulling out his wallet. He glared at them when they made to do the same. "Let's walk back to the pub. There will probably be taxis out now." He waited for them to exit the booth then followed them out.

They walked back toward the pub where they could see people getting into taxis.

"I'm going to tell you guys one thing, right now. I will not tolerate anything except honesty. If you like something, or don't like something, if you want to have dinner with me or don't want to have dinner with me, if you think I'm a controlling bastard or can't wait for me to tell you to suck my cock, whatever. Just be honest." He stopped two buildings down from the pub, put one hand on each of their waists, leaned in and kissed Richard, long and hard.

Taryn thought she might pass out, she was so turned on. She had seen men kiss before, and it had been pleasant to watch, but this, this was so clearly foreplay and not just for the guys. Despite the fact that they were the ones kissing, she didn't feel left out. Caleb's hand inched its way higher, his thumb coming to rest just under her breast. Her breathing deepened, as if her breast was trying to coax his hand higher.

Then Caleb's mouth fastened on hers. She tasted him, warm and hard, with a hint of Richard underneath. He fucked her mouth, plunging his tongue in and out and around. Normally she hated that in a first kiss, but the last hour had been working her up to this and she was *so* ready. He broke off and she couldn't suppress a whimper. He chuckled warmly, his hands going up to cup each of their necks. Then his look grew stern.

"You two can sleep together, but no sex until you talk to me, or you decide you're not going to have dinner with me. I'm not going to be the only one not getting any, clear?" He quirked one brow until they both gave small nods.

"Be safe going home. I hope you answer my call." Then he was gone.

Taryn grabbed Richard's hand and they walked to a waiting cab.

Chapter Two

೫

Richard and Taryn woke up in Richard's bed early the next morning. Or rather, Taryn woke up and made sure Richard soon followed. He moaned. Taryn fetched him a glass of water and a couple Tylenol.

"I love you. Thank you. But this is all your fault, don't forget." He swallowed the Tylenol and finished the glass of water.

"True, but look what happened. Isn't that worth a bit of a headache?"

"Asked the brat who doesn't get hangovers."

She leaned down and kissed him. "I'll go make you a BLT."

Richard sighed and rolled over. He was so lucky to have her in his life. They had talked once, maybe a year ago, about the fact that they were both still looking for Mister Perfect, but that they were losing hope such a man existed for each of them. They decided if they reached a certain age, they would just go ahead and marry each other and have kids. They'd never chosen what an appropriate age might be.

He pushed out of bed and jumped into the shower. He made it quick, threw on sweats and a t-shirt, and arrived at the kitchen just as she put a plate down on the table. "Thanks, sweetie, I really appreciate it."

She sat down with her own sandwich and they ate.

"Ricky, do you think…I mean, could we be…er…do you think Caleb thought we were…" She paused. "I liked him, a lot, but he was awfully…bossy."

"You mean domineering. Or rather, *dominating*."

"Yeah, I guess so. That's what he was implying, right? That he likes to dominate in bed? That he wants his partners to be submissive."

They both mulled that over.

"Do you think we could be submissives? Wouldn't we already know that about ourselves if we were?"

He thought about it for a minute. "I think it's just never been much of an issue for us before. You've never met a man who has wanted to…dominate." He watched her face for a reaction but she was carefully keeping impassive. "So it hasn't really made a difference. But then again, you haven't stopped looking for 'something more'. For me, gay guys tend to be a bit more conscious of the whole label thing. Like the fact that it really bugs some of them that I like sleeping with you."

He reached over and held her hand, plying his fingers through hers. "Plus, they tend to be a bit more literal with the whole top and bottom thing, which I don't really get. I mean, I like to do both, I can't imagine limiting myself to just one."

"So you've had lovers who expected you to always be in charge? How did that go?"

"Fine for a while, but then it got kind of tiring." He thought it through, did some calculations. "I've never lasted in that role more than a couple of months."

"And you've had lovers who expected you to be submissive. How did *that* go?"

He grinned. "*That* depended on the guy. Some were too controlling, especially outside the bedroom. Some were just not very good at it, at least in my opinion. It didn't feel, I don't know, natural, I guess."

"It just seems like, at our ages, we should know something like that about ourselves. But maybe we're not, maybe we're just reacting to Caleb that way, 'cause it sure as hell made me hot."

"Maybe so, but what's bad about that? We, of all people, know that getting wrapped up in labels is ridiculous. We can consider the labels guidelines, but that doesn't mean we always have to color inside of those lines. Just remember, we're always talking about how we're looking for something different, some*one* different, we just didn't know what."

"So, it seems that while we've been perfectly happy without it, that doesn't mean we couldn't give it a try."

"Well, not perfectly happy. Mostly happy. Maybe this is what we need to try in order to find perfectly happy."

"Huh."

"Yeah."

They washed the dishes and went into the living room, curling up together on the couch. Taryn opened her book and Richard started to read the newspaper.

"Taryn."

"Ricky."

"Do you think he'll call?"

"Do we want him to call?" Her voice was barely a whisper. She looked at him. "Are we asking for trouble here? Risking our relationship for the sake of a stranger, just because he's so damn sexy?"

"Have you ever reacted that way to someone you've just met? Because I haven't, and I'd like to explore what that might mean. Maybe it will crash and burn, but then again, maybe it won't. If it does, we'll still have each other, just as we always have."

She nodded. "Well, I hate to bring it up, but it certainly seems like it helped take your mind off work. How are you feeling about that?"

Richard put the newspaper down, rested his head back on the couch and closed his eyes. "Damn, Taryn, that sweet little boy. His body was so broken. They said the driver was drunk. I wasn't even any help. The ER staff was working on him, I just sat there with his mom, and she's beside herself with guilt, which is ridiculous. They worked on him for two hours, and then he was gone."

Taryn put her arms around him and Richard let himself cry. It had been so hard sitting with Elsie Jones at the ER, trying to keep her hopeful but also prepared for the worst. The poor woman had finally collapsed and been sedated, just after her ex-husband had arrived. Her mother and father were there to help her and to start the arrangements, so Richard had called Taryn and she had talked him into meeting her at the bar.

He had resolutely put all thoughts of little Matt Jones out of his head once they started drinking. He had concentrated on the music, the food, the drink and the lady. Then they had met Caleb, and it was that much easier to focus on the moment, on the lust rushing through him, the excitement, the nervousness. Hell, not so much nervousness as downright fear. He had never been so strongly attracted to someone so quickly before. At first he had to fight off a feeling of jealousy as the man's eyes had devoured Taryn's delicious curves, but then that gaze had focused on him.

He had never thought about having a threesome with Taryn, but he was sure thinking about it now. They had such a good thing together, sometimes he wished they could just get married and start getting on with the rest of their lives. Maybe have kids. But while they loved each other, they had each always wanted something more, had never stopped looking for it.

Richard sat back, wiping his eyes. Taryn kissed his cheek, then laid her head on his shoulder. She was so important to him and he could always count on her to be there for him. "Let's take a walk."

The early September heat was stuffy, so they walked slowly to a park in the neighborhood, watching the kids playing soccer for a while. Thoughts of Matt and Elsie Jones had him watching the parents, hoping they understood and appreciated this gift of watching their children run and play.

"Do you think he'll call?" Taryn asked him, her voice uncharacteristically small.

Richard drew in a deep breath, letting it out slowly. "I think he will. He seems like the kind of guy who knows what he wants. I just don't know if he wants a quick, one-time thing, or something longer lasting. Hell, I don't even know which of those I want."

Taryn nodded. "It's too early to say if there's enough there for long term. We just have to be willing to risk that one or more of us will want long term, but not all of us."

"Or that sex with a guy is something he likes to try once in a while, but he really wants a relationship with you, and I'll be the guy standing by the side watching it all happen, after I've gotten a dose of how good it could be."

"That could go the same way with me." She sighed. "I guess we just have to see what happens. At the very least, I trust you to do your best not to hurt me."

Richard put his arm around her shoulders. "Yeah, me too. Holy hell, though, I want him so badly."

"Yeah, me too. I'm already way more attracted to him than the last guy I dated. Other than you, I mean," she added with a smile. "And I don't just mean physically, either, although he's sexy as hell."

"The last guy you dated. Let's see, that's the one you broke up with because he called his mom every day."

"Well, yeah. But seriously, *every* day. Sometimes more often."

"Uh-huh. And the guy before that lasted what? A week?"

"He was always telling me what to do. You know how much I hate that. For crying out loud, he told me to go to the bathroom before the movie started so I wouldn't have to get up while it was playing."

Richard laughed, remembering. "I can't decide if you're too picky or if you just have lousy taste in men. With notable exceptions, of course."

"Of course," she agreed wryly.

They walked back to the house and Taryn gathered her things to go home. She showed him how to work the three-way calling feature on his telephone, just in case, then kissed him goodbye.

Richard cleaned the house a bit then decided on a nap.

The phone woke him an hour later, not the ring he had designated as being from the office answering service.

"Hello," he got out then cleared his throat, rubbing his eyes with his hands.

"Richard." Caleb's voice was strong and sure and sexy as hell.

"Caleb."

"Were you sleeping?"

"Mmm. Yeah. Sorry, just taking a nap. Taryn doesn't do sleeping in no matter how late she gets to bed."

"Is she there?"

"No, she went home a few hours ago."

"Did you guys talk about me?"

"A little bit. Do you want me to call her? She showed me how to do the three-way calling thing."

Caleb laughed. "No, I've got it. Hold on." He went away for a minute then clicked back over. Richard could hear the phone ringing, as well as Caleb's breathing.

"Hello?"

"Taryn."

"Caleb. Hi, how are you?" She sounded nervous, talking faster than normal.

"I'm...anxious. I want to see you both again. I've had a hard-on since last night and it doesn't seem to want to go away."

Richard cleared his throat again. "Maybe we could help you with that."

"I had hoped maybe you could. Are you available for dinner tonight?"

They both agreed they were.

"I could make something here," Richard offered.

"No, we're going to go somewhere nice. I'll wine you and dine you and we can learn a bit more about each other. In public. So I'm not too tempted to tear all your clothes off and attack you both."

"Uh," Richard said.

"Aah," Taryn said.

"How does Indigo's at seven sound?"

Taryn's "Okay" was a whisper and Richard had to force away the image of her looking breathy and nervous and ready to be ravished.

"Sounds perfect," he managed.

They all hung up and he lay back down, his hand going to his cock. He pictured Taryn on her knees sucking Caleb's cock. Richard groaned, shocked at how arousing he found the scene. He put himself behind Taryn, snuggling his cock into the crack of her ass, leaning over her so that his face was close to her mouth, breathing in Caleb's scent.

He could reach his hands around and gently work her breasts, then surprise her with a quick pinch on the nipples. She would groan and that would vibrate up Caleb's dick, maybe push him into orgasm. As she was milking him clean, he would put his fingers into Taryn's pussy, sure that it would be sopping wet. He would only need to pump her once or twice, caress her clit, and she would go off.

Richard erupted, spilling his seed onto his stomach. He sighed, hoping his imagination was not better than reality.

Chapter Three

🔊

Caleb looked around as he entered Indigo's. It was a restaurant he did not indulge in often, but one he liked very much and treated himself to when he was in a good mood.

"Caleb, it's nice to see you again," the hostess said with a sultry smile when he walked in.

"Melody, always a pleasure." He waited while she used the phone to call Andrew, one of the restaurant's co-owners.

She hung up as a couple opened the door behind him. "If you don't mind waiting a minute, Andrew said he would show you to your table himself."

Nodding, he stepped out of the way to wait for his client and friend. He'd worked closely with Andrew while modernizing the restaurant's security system

The small, middle-aged man didn't keep Caleb waiting but appeared quickly to escort him to the back of the restaurant.

"Business looks good," Caleb commented with a look around.

"It is, excellent in fact. I'm guessing you're here for a date, since you requested this table?" he asked with a raised eyebrow.

"First date," Caleb confirmed with a grin, "so make me look good."

"As if you need any help," Andrew scoffed. "Is your date bringing a chaperone?" He indicated the three place settings.

"Sort of," was all the answer he wanted to give right now. "Everything working out all right with Tom?"

After the initial setup of the security system Caleb had handed the account off to one of his best employees.

"Of course, my friend. You would have heard from me by now if there was a problem. But we can talk business some other night, I'll leave you to your date for now. I'm glad you chose us for your special night."

Caleb shook his hand and turned to the table. He chose the chair in the back, wanting Taryn and Richard to be seated on either side of him. As much as he liked the bond they shared, he didn't want them falling back on it when they became nervous. He chuckled to himself, because he had plans to make them both nervous tonight. When was the last time he'd looked forward to a date so much?

By the time he got home last night, Caleb had stopped examining his surprising feelings. During the drive he had vacillated between cursing himself for not pushing them for more that night, and plans for drawing this out, letting it build until they were all crazy with the need to be together. He had finally decided that he would ask them to dinner, make the whole evening foreplay.

This morning, he had only allowed himself a moment to wonder if they would be receptive to his calls, but he was not a man who doubted himself often. For many years in the military his safety and those of his teammates had depended on his ability to read people, as well as situations, to reach a conclusion and come to a decision. Still, he'd been unprepared for the punch to his gut at hearing their voices on the phone. Hearing the combination of anticipation and apprehension in both of them.

Caleb had taken a long shower, letting the various shower heads pound into him as he imagined Richard on his hands and knees, taking everything Caleb had to give him, while Richard noisily slurped and sucked at Taryn's sweet pussy, her eyes glued to Caleb's. His orgasm had seemed to be never-ending and his knees had been weak by the time he was finished.

Adjusting himself under the table, Caleb took a drink of his water. He looked to the entrance and saw Richard walking toward the table, alone. Where last night he had looked like a professional after work cutting loose, tonight he looked like a man dressed to impress. His charcoal suit set off his brown hair and eyes, his boyish good looks now more sophisticated.

Caleb rose, his eyes steady on the younger man's, resisting the urge to smile as Richard blushed and dropped his gaze. Caleb reached his hand out and Richard took it, flicking his eyes back up to Caleb's. He smiled and caught his breath as Caleb's other hand rested on his hip for just a moment, before moving to his back and guiding him to a chair.

They heard the sound of heels clicking on the wood floor and Caleb looked up to see Taryn approaching. Her dress was sophisticated but undeniably sexy, nearly reaching her knees but faithfully showcasing her hourglass figure. Her hair was swept up, leaving tendrils that his fingers ached to wrap around. Her eyes bounced briefly between them before settling on Caleb's. Her lips parted on a sharp inhale when he stepped toward her. He leaned in slowly, brushing her cheek with a kiss then putting his nose to the sweet spot just below her ear and inhaling deeply.

"Mmmm," he murmured, again having to hide his smile as she gave a small gasp. He settled her in the chair across from Richard and took his own seat. The waiter asked if they were ready to make their drink orders.

Richard grimaced, reassuring Caleb that last night's heavy drinking was not a usual occurrence.

Taryn laughed at him then switched her attention to the waiter who was watching her with interest, though she didn't appear to notice. Caleb restrained his impulse to redirect her attention.

"I'll have a Manhattan please."

Caleb resisted the urge to narrow his eyes as the waiter's interest lingered on her.

"Richard?" Caleb prompted.

"I'll take a light beer." He smiled when he said it and this time it was Caleb who had to force his attention back to the waiter.

"Guinness, thanks."

"I'll give you time to look at the menus," the waiter suggested and left.

"Richard. Taryn."

They smiled back. "Caleb," they answered in unison.

"I'm glad you came."

Taryn pulled her lips between her teeth then blushed when Caleb's gaze narrowed on them. "We were glad you called."

"You didn't really think I would be able to stay away, did you?" he asked. She ducked her head shyly.

"We weren't sure how much of last night was real and how much was wishful thinking," Richard said.

Caleb's lips quirked. "You were pretty drunk."

Richard's face went sad and he looked down at the table. "I lost a patient yesterday. Seven-year-old boy." He swallowed hard.

Caleb and Taryn both reached out to lay their hands on his. "It's not the first time...it's just hard." He gave a bitter laugh. "I thought family practice would be easier, after I did my ER rotation. But in the ER, you don't really get to know them. This kid, he's been mine for four years. I saw him through the measles, a broken arm—" He broke off. "I'm sorry." He shook his head.

Caleb brought his free hand up to Richard's neck, giving a gentle squeeze.

"Don't apologize. It's to your credit that you care about your patients. It's hard for you, I'm sure, but I have no doubt it makes you a better doctor."

Taryn smiled proudly. "Richard is a fantastic doctor. His patients love him. The mother called him when she got to the hospital, even though the ER was taking care of her boy. He stayed there for hours, making sure she had all the updates he could get, making sure they were doing everything they could. It was a difficult day."

"I'm okay," Richard said, picking up his menu, obviously wanting to drop the subject.

"This is a nice restaurant," Taryn commented as she looked at the menu.

"It's one of my favorites." Caleb put his menu down. "I'm sure you'll find something you like."

"I think it's going to be more of a case of too many choices," Richard said.

The waiter arrived with their drinks but left when he saw that they weren't ready to order. Caleb waited until Taryn put her menu down.

"What work do you do, Taryn?"

"I have a coffee shop, near the college. It's called Grounded." She glanced at him. "I don't actually like coffee, so I figured I wouldn't get into too much trouble sampling my wares that way."

Caleb laughed. "Good thinking. Have you been there long?"

"I bought a coffee shop that had been around a while and was a bit stale about eight years ago. The owners had been putting off retiring for a long time before they finally gave in. I updated the look, modernized the equipment and the menu, put in wi-fi and a couple of rental computers, tried to make it more college friendly."

Richard looked up from his menu. "It's a great shop. I spent a huge portion of medical school in there. When our practice was looking for a new building last year I managed to maneuver them into one across the street. Our coffee habit has skyrocketed but we aren't complaining." He smiled at Taryn with pride.

Caleb raised his eyebrow. "Considering you described yourselves as 'kind of shy' and 'think most people are irritating', you both seem to be in jobs that work with the public," he pointed out.

Taryn frowned. "Well, it's different when you can kick them out if they annoy you."

Caleb laughed and Taryn blushed.

The waiter came to take their orders. When he left, Caleb decided it was time to redirect the conversation for a while.

"Richard." Caleb's voice was hard and strong and Richard's eyes went a little bit wide.

"Caleb."

"I know you didn't have sex with Taryn after you left last night. Did you masturbate?"

Richard nodded his head but Caleb just kept looking at him until he answered. "Yes."

"What did you think about?"

Richard shifted and glanced around the area.

"Richard." Caleb added a bite to his words, bringing Richard's focus back to his face, which he kept stern. The other man swallowed hard.

"I, uh..." He cleared his throat. "I imagined Taryn sucking you off."

Caleb's face softened in approval, his voice less harsh. "And what were you doing while she did that?"

Caleb could hear Taryn's breathing picking up, matching Richard's.

"I played with her breasts and her pussy. I pinched her nipples and her moaning made you come. I brought her to orgasm by playing with her clit. I licked you, next to her mouth, so that I could taste your cum."

Caleb nodded without smiling and turned to look at Taryn. Her eyes had gone a bit glazed and she was biting her lower lip, sucking it into her mouth.

"Taryn."

She blinked, moved her gaze from Richard's to his.

"Taryn," he said again when she didn't answer.

She blushed again, snapping back to the conversation. "Caleb."

"Did you masturbate after you left last night?"

"Yes, Caleb."

He smiled, liking very much the way she said that.

"Tell us what you imagined."

She opened her mouth, shut it, opened it again. She looked down at the table, watched his hands instead of his face.

"You were both holding me, between you, my legs around Richard's waist, your hands on my hips. He was fucking me, using his hands to hold my..." she broke off, took a drink.

"He held me open for you and you filled me up." She stopped again.

"Go on," he ordered.

"Ricky was kissing me and you were nibbling on my shoulder, my ear. Then you guys kissed, over my shoulder, and I came."

The waiter chose that perfect moment to bring the appetizers to the table. When he left, Caleb asked them how they had met. They were taken off guard again by the switch in conversation, but told him about meeting in college. He let them relax into the more casual discussion, telling them about the security firm that he and his partner ran, about the challenges of opening a second office there, dealing with new clients, hiring new employees. They had a lot to talk about, no awkward silences as they ate their delicious meals. He was impressed by them, would be happy to be their friend if it were not for the incredible sexual tension gripping them all. No way would he be happy being anything less than their lover, for now.

When they ordered dessert and the waiter had left again, Caleb sat back and looked at them both. They were relaxed and smiling again, comfortable with each other, comfortable with him. He asked them about their homes and was pleased they all lived relatively close to the restaurant. One of the benefits of living in a smallish college town. While they ate dessert, Taryn talked about her apartment above the coffee shop that she had fixed up once the shop was put together to her satisfaction.

"Decorating has been slow and interesting, because I have no sense of style whatsoever." She laughed at herself then blushed when Caleb leaned over to look at her very stylish dress and raised an eyebrow at her.

She gave her best haughty look and said, "Richard bought this for me for my birthday." She managed to hold the look for two whole seconds before giggling.

"True, and her place has great style, mostly because she listened to me on pretty much everything."

"What about your place then?"

Richard grimaced. "Well now, that's different. I have my grandmother's house. I keep meaning to renovate it but it's going to be a big project. Actually, I'm thinking of selling it to my cousin Mark and letting him deal with it."

Caleb nodded his understanding. "Family and real estate can be tricky. I'm renting because my brother is trying to guilt me into moving into our parents' house. Right now we have renters in there, since my parents gave it to us and moved into a retirement community in Florida. It's too much house for one person, though I like it and the neighborhood. It needs work, too."

Taryn rested her chin on her hand. "So why doesn't your brother and his wife live there? Don't they have kids?"

"One and hoping for more, which wouldn't fill up the house but comes a lot closer than me on my own. But Lisa's father built their house for them as a wedding present. He's a contractor."

"Yeah, I suppose that would be hard to give up. Where is your parents' house?"

"Ridgewood Heights."

"Oh, that's a great neighborhood. It's behind the coffee shop."

"Well, much as I like it, I'm not in any hurry to try to update its style. Although since we have a confirmed decorator in our midst, maybe I could gather some advice."

"I trusted him on everything but the bed sheets," Taryn laughed. "I drew the line at black satin."

"But you don't mind enjoying the ones at my house," Richard pointed out.

They all laughed until Caleb, keeping his voice even, slid in with, "Why don't you show me?"

Richard and Taryn both stopped laughing and looked at each other, then at him.

"Okay," Richard answered, his expression nervous but determined.

"Did you guys drive here?"

Taryn shook her head and Richard said, "I took a taxi."

"Me too."

Caleb smiled, pleased. He stood and they followed. He began to lead Taryn out but she glanced back at the table.

"Caleb, we haven't gotten the bill."

He smiled at her. "Don't worry."

She frowned at him. "Caleb, we don't expect..."

He interrupted her with a light kiss. "Don't worry," he said again, when he had pulled back. He ushered them outside to where his SUV sat waiting at the curb.

When they arrived at Richard's house, Caleb complimented it. It was small but charming and obviously well maintained, despite his earlier comments. Caleb grabbed a small bag from the SUV.

As Richard unlocked the door and motioned them inside, Caleb took Taryn's hand and gave it a reassuring squeeze. She held on to him tightly while they walked in. He let her go with a gentle push to the couch and indicated that Richard should join her. He sat in the matching chair next to it, turned so that he was facing them.

"I told you that I believe very strongly that we need to be completely honest with each other. That doesn't just mean not lying, but in communicating fully. It's pretty obvious I very much want to fuck you both tonight. I think I can assume you're both on the same page, as far as that goes."

He waited for them to nod, noticed they were holding hands, gripping each other tightly.

"I need you to tell me if you have any specific expectations from this, and if you have any limits. You know that I am a Dominant, I like to be in charge in the bedroom. Not necessarily every night, but a good portion of the time. I am not into pain, although I can be persuaded to indulge some if you're into that." They both winced a little and he figured he was safe on that score. Hurting people, even when they wanted him to, was not how he got off. He much preferred torturing them with pleasure.

"I'm just not sure how I'm going to feel about that. I've never tried it and I for sure don't like people telling me what to do in my everyday life. But nothing you've done has turned me off so far, so I'm willing to give it a try." Taryn looked nervous but relaxed somewhat when he smiled.

"Fair enough."

Richard cleared his throat. "I'm definitely not into whips and collars, but I don't mind, um," he glanced at Taryn, "being tied up occasionally."

Caleb nodded his agreement, happy that they were opening up. He kept his tone light, wanting them to be comfortable talking about these things. "It's important to understand that there is no black and white. There are levels to everything. When I say I don't like to give pain, that means I don't do whips, but doesn't mean that a nip here or there, or a good nipple twist, doesn't have its place, as does a nice spanking when someone earns it. If at any time you're uncomfortable with something, if I've misjudged what you want or are capable of handling, you have to feel like you can tell me that."

"Like a safe word?" Richard asked.

"That's the idea, yes, but I don't plan on doing anything intense enough where that would be necessary. If you tell me to stop, I'll stop. If you want to slow down, or pause to talk about something, that's okay, too. I expect to earn your trust." He waited, made sure they were with him. "Now, what else? Anything you particularly want to try, or want to avoid?"

Taryn seemed to be debating something with herself so Caleb looked at Richard, who glanced back at Taryn.

"I've never done anal with Taryn, and I don't imagine she has with anyone else, either."

Caleb looked at her, could see that this was what she had been debating in her head. "Your fantasy was just that, a fantasy."

She nodded, squared her shoulders. "I think I would like to try it, to have two men, at once, but not tonight. I think it would be better as a gradual thing, don't you think?" She looked at Caleb, as if worried he might be mad.

"That's not a problem. There are plenty of things we can do besides that, and plenty of ways we can introduce it gradually to make the journey as enjoyable as the end result."

Taryn relaxed a little, then nudged Richard's arm, gesturing to Caleb.

Richard mumbled, "I have a strong gag reflex." But Caleb heard him. He nodded at the man, encouraging him to continue, careful not to laugh at how cute Richard was.

Richard just shrugged. "It's always been a problem."

Caleb made no reply and waited for more.

"Do you have any, uh, fetishes, or something, that we should know about?" Taryn asked him.

He gave her a pleased smile. "Good question. Obviously, being in charge is a big turn-on for me. I like to see my lover bound at my mercy sometimes. I'm a big fan of using toys. For the most part though, there is nothing that I think you would consider weird or a fetish."

When they had all remained quiet for another moment, Caleb stood up.

"We're all going to take a potty break and meet back here. Rick, you get us some water from the kitchen. I've got condoms. Anything else?" They both shook their heads and headed out in different directions, Caleb using the master bath so he could check it and the bedroom out. They met back up a few minutes later, in the living room.

"Excellent," Caleb said. "Let's take this to the bedroom."

Chapter Four

ഔ

Taryn couldn't remember being this excited or nervous entering into a new sexual relationship. This afternoon she'd been worried Caleb was only interested in a one-night stand, but now she couldn't imagine any of them getting this out of their systems any time soon. The trick was going to be making sure that when the time came, they all parted amicably.

The conversation in the living room had made her a little uncomfortable. She'd never had such a discussion with a lover, let alone a potential lover, even Ricky. They'd just bumbled along, learning each other's likes and dislikes through trial and error. Now that she thought about it, it was stupid. If you were willing to share body fluids, surely you should be capable of discussing your wants and limits with that person, rather than risk misunderstanding. It hadn't been easy, but now that it was over she felt less nervous and more anxious. Her estimation of Caleb rose even higher.

She led the way into Richard's master bedroom, then stood to the side so that the men could enter behind her. They stepped inside and Caleb closed the bedroom door. For some reason that struck Taryn as very important, like he was saying from now on they were in his territory and they better be prepared to do what he said. She shivered.

"Richard. Taryn. You're mine now. You understand?"

They both nodded.

"Say it."

"Yes, Caleb," they answered simultaneously. Though his expression didn't change, Taryn could tell he was pleased by the response.

"Taryn, undress Rick." She didn't hesitate. She turned to Richard and started to work on his tie. Their eyes met and she saw excitement with an edge of nervousness, and gave him a tiny smile, knowing he probably saw the same in her. Her fingers shook and she jerked, nearly choking Richard when Caleb came up behind her and rested his hands on her shoulders. He squeezed gently and she realized she'd stopped moving. She resumed her task, pulled the tie loose and began unbuttoning Richard's shirt.

Caleb's hands moved to the zipper at the back of her dress and she had to concentrate very hard to get the last of the buttons open. She used her hands to push the shirt off Richard's shoulders, sliding them down his arms, taking strength from the familiar feel of him. The sleeves caught at the wrists because she hadn't unbuttoned the cuffs, and she growled in frustration. Her breathing was heavy, and so was Richard's. She glanced at him and saw that he was looking over her shoulder at Caleb with heat in his eyes. It was a little strange to see that heat directed at someone else, especially when she was standing between them, but a shiver of excitement raced through her.

Taryn felt cool air at her back and realized that Caleb had brought her zipper down without actually touching her. She fumbled with Richard's cuffs and finally freed his shirt just as Caleb slid his hands into her dress at her waist. His skin was warm with small calluses, which raised goose bumps on her arms. She realized he wasn't moving, probably because she had stopped as well. She forced her hands to Richard's belt and Caleb resumed his upward path, his fingers curled to her sides, his thumbs tracing her spine.

She ripped the belt off in record time and attacked the button and zipper, while Caleb remained unhurried. Looking up, she saw a bead of sweat roll down Richard's temple and she was impressed by his restraint at standing still while she and Caleb were able to touch. She would have liked to touch more but it surprised her that she had no desire to ignore

Caleb's directions and hurry things along. Apparently Richard felt the same because his hands remained at his sides.

Taryn eased a hand into Richard's slacks to cup his enormous erection so that she could pull the zipper down safely. Richard's dick practically leapt into her hand and she definitely was tempted to say hello, but Caleb had paused again. When she removed her hand as soon as the zipper was down, he moved on to her bra. She held her breath as he traced the band with his thumbs, then continued on his journey, his fingers curling in so that his knuckles brushed the sides of her breasts.

She pushed Richard's pants down, making sure his boxers went too. They dropped to his feet and she stood still, quivering, while Caleb's hands curved over her shoulders and sent her dress down to puddle at her feet.

"Kick them away, Rick," Caleb said, his voice only slightly betraying his arousal.

Richard did as he was told, toeing off his shoes, then kicking them, his slacks and his boxers away, so that he was left only in his socks, which he quickly removed.

Caleb tapped Taryn's right thigh with his fingers and she lifted her leg. She could feel him gently maneuvering her dress away from her foot. He tapped her other ankle and she switched legs. Her dress now gone, she was left in her bra, panties, garter, hose and heels. Richard glanced down at her and smiled. He started to reach his hand to her, then stopped, his eyes widening. He looked over her shoulder again and dropped his hand.

Caleb came around from behind Taryn, looking Richard up and down very slowly. He came in close so that he was touching both of their thighs with his, laying one hand on Taryn's bra strap, idly caressing the flesh underneath. He leaned in and kissed Richard, resting his other hand on the curve of Richard's lower back. Taryn's heart felt as if it was going to beat right out of her chest. She licked her lips and whimpered as Caleb feasted. She could tell the moment that

Richard came to his senses enough to kiss back. The heat ratcheted up a notch and Richard's hand came up to rest on Caleb's chest.

Caleb backed off from the kiss, giving little mini kisses until Richard's eyes opened again and he was steady on his feet.

"I've been wanting to do that since you walked into the restaurant," Caleb said.

Richard licked his lips. "I've been wanting you to do that since you did it last night."

Caleb smiled then turned to look at Taryn.

She'd dressed in the fancy lingerie, not sure if it was making her look sexy or just fat, but Caleb's eyes said that she had managed sexy just fine. That, coupled with Richard's reaction a minute ago, gave her the courage she needed to keep her hands where they were, even though she wanted to hug them to herself. She fisted them to keep them still. Caleb apparently recognized this victory, running his hands down her arms in approval. He wrapped his long fingers around her wrists and brought her arms up away from her body. She relaxed in his grip, no longer having to concentrate on keeping herself still.

"Richard, we're going to have to reward Taryn for dressing so nicely for us."

Nodding, Richard reached a finger out to trace the lacy bra cup. "Seems your style doesn't need all that much help after all, sweetie."

Taryn studied Richard's face, worried that he might be jealous that she had never worn such a thing for him before, but his eyes were glued to her body and he seemed perfectly happy with what he was seeing now.

Caleb transferred one of her wrists to Richard then led her to the bed. He backed her into it so that she was standing with her thighs pressed against the mattress.

"Rick, get up on the bed behind her and hold her hands for me."

Richard complied, holding her wrists so that they were behind her, her elbows bent. The position thrust her breasts toward Caleb and her nipples hardened in expectation. Caleb hooked his finger into the cup of her bra, drawing it down until it was below her hard peak, which he promptly took into his mouth, sucking gently. She jerked, then jerked again as she felt Richard's firm hold. Her heart was going to burst from her chest, it was beating so fast.

"Breathe," Caleb reminded her, releasing one nipple before moving to the other. He wet that one thoroughly as well, then stepped back to view his handiwork. He smiled, then leaned down again and blew a cool stream on both breasts. Taryn gasped. Caleb drew in close, chafing her with his hard chest, reaching behind her to work the bra clasp. He stepped away, pushing the fabric down her arms as far as it would go while Richard still held her.

Hard hands cupped her breasts and his thumbs flicked her nipples, causing electric sparks to shoot through her body. Taryn moaned, leaning forward, only to be brought up short by Richard's hands on her wrists and the bra pulled tight across her stomach. Caleb reached a hand over her shoulder and brought Richard forward for another kiss, rewarding him for his hard work and restraint. Squeezed between them, she didn't think she'd ever felt so alive, so hot, so ready. Her skin was so sensitized she felt every point of contact from both men and ached for more.

The kiss almost distracted her from the feel of Caleb's hands sliding back down her body, his fingers untying the tiny bows at the sides of her panties, which were surely soaked through. Caleb pulled back from the kiss, leaving Richard panting in Taryn's ear. Richard leaned forward, warming her back as he looked over her shoulder and down her body. His warm breath caressed her chest and she tilted her head to rest against his. They both watched as Caleb squatted down to the floor, eased the panties to her feet, and helped her step out of them. He looked directly at her crotch and smiled, then blew gently on her curls, which were soaking wet. He stood up abruptly and Taryn moaned in denial.

"Rick, you can let go of her now. I want you to sit up against the pillows at the headboard, legs wide, so Taryn can sit between them." As soon as Richard let go of her hands Taryn brought them forward, letting the bra fall off. Not to cover herself, but to touch Caleb. She wanted that damn shirt off, so she could see him.

Caleb immediately caught them up again.

"Naughty girl, that's not going to do at all. Go sit on the bed, make sure your ass is hugged in nice and tight to Rick's balls." She turned to get on the bed, wiggling her ass in his direction as she crawled to Richard. Richard's eyes were fastened on her breasts as they swayed toward him.

Caleb's hand smacked her behind. It didn't hurt but it startled the hell out of her. She looked back over her shoulder at him, but he just quirked his brow. She rolled her eyes. She had to admit, she had pretty much asked for that. Richard's amused smile in no way diminished the heat in his eyes. She stuck her tongue out at him and he bit his lips to keep from laughing out loud. She turned around and sat in front of Richard, scooting back until she was tight against him. He was a hard heat at her back and she had no questions about how excited he was. She looked back at Caleb.

He had taken off his tie and was climbing onto the bed. He nudged one knee between hers, the other next to Richard's, so that he was kneeling over both of them.

"I want to see you naked," she said to Caleb, trying not to pout.

"I second that," Richard added, his hands coming to rest on her thighs, thumbs moving restlessly over her skin.

"Well then, you should probably stop interrupting me." His tone was hard as he stood watching them, but Taryn was sure she saw a twinkle in his eye. She gave him a warning glare but kept her mouth shut.

"Taryn, put your hands behind Rick's neck," Caleb continued after a heartbeat.

She did as he said, then closed her eyes as he leaned into her, reaching behind Richard to tie her wrists with his tie. He smelled delicious and she missed his heat when he pulled back. She opened her eyes and watched him survey his work. He ran his hand down Richard's side, along his hip, all the way to the ankle. He lifted the ankle then placed it on the inside of Taryn's leg, pulling it out so that her legs went wider. He repeated the action with Richard's other leg. Then he put a hand on each ankle and pulled, sliding Richard down a couple of inches, taking Taryn with him. Taryn could feel Richard's heartbeat under hers, going a hundred miles a minute. She was lying more firmly against him now, his cock trapped beneath her lower back. They were both totally at Caleb's mercy, and he was still fully clothed.

"Ricky, you can use your hands however you want, but keep your legs where they are."

Richard's hands immediately went to her breasts, caressing them. She could feel his lips in her hair, his breath on her ear.

She was spread wide open to Caleb's gaze, still wearing her garter belt, stockings and heels.

"Caleb, please."

"Please what, baby?" he asked softly.

"I want to see you, touch you."

"Shhhh." He leaned in, pressing his lips to hers, but not opening them.

He retreated and she laid her head back against Richard's chest.

Caleb got off the bed and kicked off his shoes. He unbuttoned his cuffs, then his shirt. His eyes were on them, on Richard's hands playing with Taryn's breasts.

Her eyes were glued to the chest he revealed as he finally removed the damn shirt.

"Mmmm," she hummed her approval.

"Oh yeah," Richard agreed.

Caleb's lips twitched into a grin before he smoothed it out.

"You have marvelous tits," he said. "Squeeze her nipples for me, Ricky." Richard complied and Taryn's back arched, pressing her more firmly into Richard's cock. They moaned in unison.

Caleb took off his belt and unbuttoned his pants, but didn't pull the zipper down. He climbed back onto the bed, lying between their legs, his hands caressing Richard's hips, his breath hot on Taryn's pussy.

"Mmm, you smell delicious."

"She is," Richard said. He took his hands from Taryn's breasts and slid them down her body to her pussy. He used his fingers to open her folds for Caleb. Caleb murmured his approval, leaned in and ran his tongue from bottom to top.

Taryn moaned, tilting her pelvis to get more, feeling Richard's hard cock jerking under her. Richard put his finger into her hole while Caleb watched, swirled it around in her juices, then brought it out, offering it to Caleb, who sucked it into his mouth. Taryn had never been turned on with so little actual touching in her life. She felt like she might explode at any moment. Caleb lowered his head and thrust his tongue into her channel while Richard used his wet finger to caress her clit.

Taryn's head thrashed from side to side. Caleb fluttered his tongue and she came with a long moan.

Caleb raised his head and looked at them. He smiled. "Okay, we're almost ready to get started."

"Fuck," Taryn breathed.

"Eventually," Caleb answered.

He attacked her with his tongue then moved up to her clit, sucking it into his teeth. Richard's hands moved back up to her breasts, pulling gently at first, then more firmly.

Caleb slid one hand under Richard's ass, pressing him harder into Taryn's back. He brought his other hand around and slid one finger into her, followed quickly by another. Taryn would have thought it would take awhile after her orgasm to be ready again, but she felt like she was already on the edge. Caleb pumped the fingers in and out of her, in and out, then curled them up to find her G-spot. She creamed around him and he moaned his approval, which vibrated her clit.

Those now wet fingers brushed up her side and into the space between her and Richard's bodies. He gripped Richard's cock, his fingers warm and wet against the small of her back as they moved up and down in the tiny movements allowed by the limited space. Caleb's tongue went back to her passage, fucking into her in a steady rhythm. Richard's hands jerked against her breasts as he lost his own tempo and tried to work his hips beneath her.

"Rick."

"Ye-yes, Caleb?" Richard gasped.

"Taryn."

"Yes, C-Caleb," Taryn moaned. They were all breathing hard.

"I want you to come now," he said, then lowered his mouth to her clit.

Richard and Taryn cried out in unison, her orgasm going on and on, Caleb not letting up until the end, Richard's seed scalding her back.

They lay there, unmoving, exhausted, eyes closed.

Finally Taryn opened her eyes a slit.

"Caleb. What about..." She gestured vaguely in his direction.

"Don't worry," he said. "We haven't really started yet. That was just to thank you for wearing the pretty underwear."

"Holy hell."

"Yeah," said Richard. "What she said."

Caleb moved Richard's legs from hers and took off her shoes. He unhooked the garters and rolled down her stockings then held a hand out to her. Raising her bound hands over Richard's head, she offered them to him. He untied her and pulled her up and off the bed. He slid her garter belt down and she stepped out of it. Then he kissed her long and hard, wrapping his strong arms around her to support her, his chest hair brushing her sensitive nipples.

"Go start the shower."

She walked to the bathroom, looking over her shoulder to see Caleb offering a hand to Richard.

Richard could hardly believe he'd experienced such a powerful orgasm from Caleb's hand barely able to massage his dick between the press of the sexy, squirming Taryn on top of him. He got off the bed with a hand from Caleb. He put his other hand on the man's chest, admiring the flex and play of muscles, and the contrast of his own olive skin against Caleb's lighter complexion. Licking his lips, he smoothed his hand over to Caleb's nipple.

Caleb grabbed his wrist and held it away.

"Ah, ah, ah. I've got other plans for those fingers right now. I assume you have some lube handy?" he asked. Richard opened a drawer of the nightstand and pulled out a bottle. Caleb added the condoms from his pocket and set them on top of the nightstand.

Taking Richard's hand, he pulled him into the bathroom, where Taryn had the water running nice and hot. Caleb pulled his pants off and stepped to Richard and Taryn. Putting one arm around each of their waists, he leaned in, letting his very erect cock tickle their stomachs while Taryn's nipples tried to play with each of their chests. Richard rested one hand on the top of Caleb's ass, the other on Taryn's hip. He watched Caleb's face, wanting so badly to kiss the man, but waiting for Caleb's next move.

Caleb moved his hands up to cup each of their necks, and pulled them together so that they were all kissing. It was sloppy but oh-so glorious. Richard closed his eyes, amazed at the difference in feeling Taryn's tongue versus Caleb's as they all danced together. He and Caleb both chased Taryn into her mouth, then Caleb changed direction and he and Taryn came at Richard. After a minute they all broke away, breathing hard.

"Let's clean you two up a bit."

They stepped into the shower and Taryn grabbed the bottle of shower gel. She lathered it up then placed her hands on Richard's shoulders and began running them down and around, making sure to pay particular attention to his nipples. He groaned when she gave them an extra sharp tug, then groaned again as Caleb's hands began massaging his shoulders with deep, powerful strokes.

As with the kiss, it was amazing how good it felt to experience both of their different touches on him at the same time. Taryn's sweet, feminine hands smoothing down his chest, heading for his cock, which was valiantly trying to rise to the occasion. Caleb's hard, calloused hands, kneading his muscles, then moving lower, firmly gripping the globes of his ass.

Richard reached for the shower gel and worked up some lather. He massaged Taryn's shoulders as Caleb had done his, then moved them down her back, trying not to jerk as her hands worked his penis back to life and Caleb's hands smoothed over his back hole. Richard gave Taryn the same treatment and she squeaked and nearly slipped.

Caleb laughed. "I think we're clean enough. Let's dry off." They each took a towel and tried to dry each other off, not accomplishing a whole lot but laughing hard. They stumbled back into the bedroom at last, mostly dry. Caleb took two of the condoms and handed one to Richard. They covered themselves quickly. Caleb picked up the lube.

"Richard, hands and knees, on the bed."

Richard heard Taryn gasp and angled his head as he climbed onto the bed to see her face. Anticipation gleamed from her eyes and she was pulling her lower lip into her mouth. She was watching him and the heat in her eyes made his blood burn.

"Taryn, give him your pussy."

Taryn levered herself onto the bed and maneuvered so that he could reach her comfortably.

Caleb put his hand on Richard's back. "Don't let her come." His hand moved to Richard's cock. "And don't you come." He began pumping, slow and sure. Richard thought his eyes would roll up into his head, but then Caleb stopped. He slapped Richard's ass, making him jump.

"You going to leave Taryn out of this?"

Richard realized he had been concentrating on what Caleb was doing and abandoned Taryn. He immediately put his face down and gave her a long lick in apology. She whimpered, then moaned as he found her clit and fluttered it with the tip of his tongue. He moved to her pussy and thrust his tongue in as far as he could just as Caleb put one lubed finger up his ass.

Richard moaned, which caused Taryn to shriek. Caleb laughed. Richard was so focused on pleasuring Taryn and enjoying what Caleb was doing to him that he almost let Taryn come. He jerked back just as Caleb thrust another finger home.

"Caleb!" he shouted.

"Richard!" Taryn wailed.

Caleb scissored his fingers inside Richard's ass for a minute, then backed out.

"Come here."

Richard turned around and found Caleb sitting back against the pillows at the headboard. He spread his legs and fisted his cock, which was red and glistening with pre-cum.

"Bring me that ass," Caleb growled, and Richard hurried to comply. He turned around and offered himself to Caleb, who used his hands to guide Richard home. Wishing he could watch the other man's face, he closed his eyes and concentrated on the hand caressing his hip, the strong thighs quivering just slightly beneath him. As he seated himself fully, Caleb brought his arms around to hug him closer, deeper, and kissed his way up Richard's neck.

"You're so tight, so perfect," Caleb murmured into his ear.

Ah fuck, it felt soooo good. Caleb's cock was thick, stretching him oh-so nicely. Had he ever been filled so completely? He looked up to see Taryn watching them, her mouth open and panting, her fingers stealing down to her pussy. Caleb must have seen her too, because he barked at her.

"Taryn!"

She jerked, her eyes flying to Caleb's face.

"My pussy," Caleb growled. Richard saw cream run down her leg. "My ass," Caleb continued, tightening his hold on Richard to force him down onto that amazing cock. He clenched his muscles and was rewarded with Caleb's groan.

"Aargh," was all Richard could say. They sat that way for a minute, without moving. Caleb's breath was loud in Richard's ear.

"Don't move, Richard. Taryn, come fill my pussy with my cock." He reached around and grabbed Richard's cock, holding it steady for Taryn who wasted no time in moving to join them. Carefully, she lowered herself down, Richard holding her steady while she worked her legs around to where they needed to be.

Her warm, snug heat surrounding his flaming cock was nearly more than he could bear when coupled with the steel that was filling him. He ground his head into Caleb's shoulder, moaning with desperation while he held the rest of himself still.

Taryn softened around him, dropping down that last little bit, then Caleb bit his ear. Richard's hips arched in surprise, sending him surging into Taryn, then he bounced back down onto Caleb. He bellowed, trying to keep from coming. Taryn leaned over and kissed Caleb, while Caleb's fingers snaked around and pinched Richard's nipple. Richard managed to arch up again, pulling a groan from Caleb as he tightened his muscles and dropped back down.

"Now."

That was all it took. Taryn came first as Caleb's other hand worked her nipple, her rippling orgasm setting Richard off. Richard's clenching brought Caleb, who had not yet come that night. They rolled onto their sides in a sweaty tangle. They rested for a minute, then Caleb went into the bathroom. He came back with a couple of washcloths and used them to clean everyone up and disposed of the condoms. He shoved at Richard until he could pull down the covers, then they all climbed underneath.

Caleb lay in the middle, with Taryn pulled snugly to his right side, her head resting on his shoulder. Richard lay on Caleb's left side, on his stomach, his head on the same pillow, his arm across Caleb's chest to rest over his heart. They were asleep within seconds.

* * * * *

"Ricky."

Caleb vaguely heard Taryn's voice, her breath tickling across his neck.

"Caleb."

He grunted and she shoved at his shoulder.

"I have to pee."

"Okay."

"I can't move."

"Okay."

"Caleb!"

Caleb cracked open an eye and found Taryn looking at him with exasperation. She'd spent half the night draped across him, a position he heartily approved of. Somehow she'd ended up between Richard and him, with Richard wrapped around her back, the man's arm coming around to rest on Caleb's hip. All of their legs were entwined. There was no way for Taryn to move without one of them giving her some room. He grinned.

"How badly do you have to go?"

She narrowed her eyes at him, reached forward and nipped his jaw. He kissed her hard, then rolled away, freeing her to get off the bed. Richard grunted in his sleep, reaching out until he felt Caleb, then snuggling in to fill the space Taryn had left. Caleb bent his elbow and propped his head on his hand, looking down at the younger man. It turned him on, knowing this very smart man, this doctor, had been his to command last night. The combination of Richard and Taryn had been more than he had ever dreamed of. He couldn't ever remember such a perfect evening, let alone such a perfect fantasy.

His cock stirred just from the thought. He heard the toilet flush and the shower turn on. Moving carefully so as not to disturb Richard, Caleb reached over to the nightstand and picked up a condom and the lube. He stroked himself while replaying the night's events in his mind and watching the sleeping man's chest rise and fall. After a couple of strokes, he sheathed himself with the condom, lubed it liberally while rehearsing his moves, then attacked. One hand grabbed Richard's wrist, yanking him so that he was fully on his stomach while Caleb's body moved to straddle him with his superior weight and strength. As Richard came awake, Caleb grabbed his other wrist, manacling both of them with his right hand, over Richard's head, Caleb's arm angling down across Richard's upper back to hold his head down on the bed.

Richard gasped but Caleb was still moving. With his free hand he reached under Richard's hip and pulled his waist up, into the cradle of Caleb's thighs. Caleb's legs moved to hold Richard's so that they were bent at the knees, spread wide and anchored at the shins to the bed. One more silent move brought Caleb's dick to Richard's hole. Caleb leaned down, draping his body over Richard's. He bit down on Richard's shoulder just as he slid home.

"Oh fuck, Caleb!" Richard shouted.

Caleb brought his left hand around to find Richard's shaft hard and leaking.

"Ricky," Caleb panted, holding still despite every nerve in his body screaming for more. He waited until Richard began pushing back into him, then thrust in and out, hard and fast. He could feel his balls tightening. He pumped the cock in his hand, pumped his dick in and out of the tight hole and came the second that Richard groaned and spurted his release. They collapsed on the bed, laughing when Taryn shook water at them.

Caleb gave Richard a light smack on the butt and got out of bed. He took a quick shower and pulled on jeans from his bag, brushed his hair and teeth. As he passed the bed he nudged the sleeping man, who ignored him. He went into the kitchen to find Taryn pouring a cup of coffee, which she held out to him. He quirked a brow at the cup but accepted it gratefully. He took a sip and moaned in pleasure.

"I'm going to have to try out your shop."

She laughed then sat at the kitchen table. "I made the coffee. I think that means you have to make the breakfast."

She looked so good sitting there, her hair still wet from the shower, her face scrubbed clean, loose pajama bottoms tied at her waist and a tiny tank top that was doing nothing to hide the nipples poking into it. He licked his lips. "I can do that." He took another large swallow of the coffee then set the mug down on the counter. "After."

He stalked to the chair and knelt between her legs, pushing her thighs apart to give him room.

"After?" she gasped as his hands spanned her waist.

"Definitely after."

He lifted her tank top and stabbed his tongue into her bellybutton. She squeaked and fisted her hands in his hair.

"Caleb."

"Taryn."

She didn't say anything further as he pushed the tank top over her head.

"Hold them for me."

Taryn blinked at him. Caleb took her hands and moved them to her breasts. She bit her lip and cupped her breasts for him. Leaning in, he used just the tip of his tongue to torture her nipples while his hands found the waistband of her pajamas and pulled them down. He bit, gently, on one puckered offering as his hands cupped her sweet ass and pulled the pants down.

"Ahrgh."

"Mmm-hmmm." Caleb moved to the other nipple and breathed on it, then watched as it, too, puckered for him.

"Squeeze."

Taryn's hands jerked in surprise then began massaging her breasts. Caleb nuzzled between the mounds, licking between her fingers. His hands moved between her thighs and he used his thumbs to part her.

"Caleb. Please." Taryn's breath was coming out in pants now, music to Caleb's ears. He gave one last swipe of his tongue.

"Move your hands down here. Show me how wet you are." He stood up and took a step back, his hands going to the button of his jeans. He paused, waiting for Taryn's brain to catch up with his orders. She had that adorable look of glazed incomprehension that he was coming to love putting on her face.

"Are you wet, baby?"

"Y-yes."

"Show me."

Her tongue darted out to wet her lips and her eyes went to his hands, which were holding still on the button of his jeans. Slowly her hands moved to her wetness. Using one to hold herself open, she used the other to circle her passage, then pulled it free. Reaching her wet fingers up to him, she offered him a taste.

Bending over to reach her fingers, Caleb kept his eyes on hers as he sucked the fingers in hard and fast, then used his tongue to explore and clean every inch of them. She tasted like woman, his woman. He pulled back, letting them go with a pop, then shucked his jeans, grabbing a condom from the pocket before moving back to her.

"Stand up."

Taryn stood, shakily, holding on to the edge of the table for support. Caleb turned her around and bent her over the table, his hand on her back positioning her how he wanted her.

"Don't move."

He brought his hands to her hips and plowed into her in one thrust. Taryn gasped and tensed, getting leverage to thrust back. Caleb put his hand on her back again and she settled. He waited until she made whimpering sounds he guessed she didn't even know she was making. Her inner walls clutched at him, and when he could stand it no longer, he held her tight and pounded into her. Lifting her hips a little higher, Caleb knew the moment he hit her sweet spot. Taryn screamed and came around his cock, and there was no holding back his own release.

Careful not to crush her into the table, Caleb kissed Taryn's neck, then got up to dispose of the condom. When he came back, she hadn't moved. He picked her up and carried her back to the bed, laying her next to Richard. She rolled over and snuggled into the sleeping man's side with a sigh. Caleb smiled and went to make breakfast.

Chapter Five

Taryn practically floated her way into Grounded Wednesday morning with a satisfied grin as she took a look around. When she'd spoken to Caleb on the phone that morning, he'd thought he might have a chance to drop by the shop today. She hoped so, looked forward to showing off her pride and joy. Besides, she just couldn't wait to see him again. They hadn't managed to mesh schedules since their amazing date Friday night and she missed him. She'd missed Richard too, having only seen him a couple of times while working.

Talking on the phone with them, separately and together, was good, but not nearly good enough. She greeted a couple of regulars and slid seamlessly into a conversation one of her employees was having with their mail carrier at the front counter. It never ceased to amaze her how comfortable she felt here. In college she had been shy and insecure for the most part. She had made a few good friends but had not been comfortable speaking up in class or attending most of the parties.

When she met Richard her junior year they had bonded instantly over a tragic server crash in the computer lab. She had been impressed by his dedication to becoming a doctor and loved to hear his stories about the town he had grown up in, his family's Italian restaurant and the mischief he and his twin had gotten into as teenagers.

As soon as Tony, their mail carrier, left, Emma narrowed her gaze on Taryn. Emma was a student at Kennington College and one of Taryn's best employees.

"What?"

"That's what I want to know. What is up with you lately? You're so…you've been so…happy."

Taryn laughed. "I wasn't happy before?"

"Not like this you weren't. What's the story? Did you win the lottery? Did you fall in love with someone, and does that mean Richard's available?"

Taryn gave her a measuring look, judging how much to tell. It was hard to keep secrets in her shop and besides, she didn't want her happiness to be a secret.

"Well, it's too soon to say if it's love, but I did meet someone and it's making me very happy. But no, that doesn't mean Richard is available. He's been very happy too, if you haven't noticed."

Emma's eyes narrowed as she ran the possibilities through. "Actually, I did notice he was in a very good mood yesterday when he stopped by. It's probably best if I don't guess. Why don't you just tell me? Start with who it is you've met."

A young couple walked in, which gave Taryn the perfect opportunity to make Emma wait, just to drag the suspense out. "You do your job well and maybe I'll reward you with the details. Do it really well and you might get to see for yourself, in a little while." She laughed and walked to the back to work in her office, ignoring the pout she knew Emma was directing at her.

Putting in two solid hours on the computer had Taryn groaning when she stood up. She stretched then answered the phone as it rang.

"Hey, sweetie, how's the grind?"

Taryn rolled her eyes at Richard's oft-used joke. "I've been stuck to the computer for a couple of hours. I'm just about to go out front and remind myself that there are people here I can boss around and that my job isn't all invoices and emails."

"I don't suppose there's anyone there I could bribe to run some mochas over here?" He almost, but not quite, succeeded in keeping the whine from his voice.

"Busy day?"

"Very. Brad got called to the hospital and Petra's on a tear about something." Brad was Richard's partner and Petra, their office manager, had become her good friend.

"Put Petra on the phone. I'll convince her to have girl's night tonight. She probably just needs a night away from Bob and the kids."

He sighed pathetically into the phone. "I will and I'm sure that will help, but it won't do much for right now."

"Yeah, yeah, stop your crying. Derek should be here by now. I'll send him over when there's a lull. He loves the tips you guys give."

"You're a lifesaver and I love you to death."

"Sure, that's what they all say." She laughed when he gave noisy kisses into the phone before transferring her to Petra.

Taryn hardly voiced her idea for girl's night before Petra jumped on the bandwagon and had it all planned out. Smiling, Taryn hung up and went to make the coffees.

Out front, Derek was helping an older gentleman on one of the computer stations and most of the couches were filled by college students. A group of ladies had pushed two of the tables together and were deep in conversation. Emma was ringing up a woman's order and Taryn gave her a second look, trying to place her. She prided herself on recognizing her repeat customers but she was pretty sure that wasn't how she knew this woman.

Her cell phone rang with the ringtone she had assigned to Caleb's number and that prompted her memory. This was Lisa, Caleb's sister-in-law. She answered the phone with a smile that she knew he would hear in her voice.

"Hey."

"Hey yourself. I'm on my way over. I just spoke to Richard and heard about his desperate need for a caffeine infusion. I told him I'd play delivery man if his tips were good enough."

"Hmm, I have a feeling your definition of what makes a good tip from Richard, and Derek's definition, are not quite the same."

She loved the sound of his laugh, loved bringing it out of him.

"I should certainly hope not or our boy is going to be in trouble." A sexy shiver shot down her spine.

"I'll get the coffees ready, but you might prefer to have Derek do the deliveries after all, if you want to talk to your sister-in-law."

"Really? Lisa's there?" He sounded surprised.

"I'm pretty sure it's her, but I only met her once, a few months ago."

"Well, I'll be there in a couple of minutes."

"I'm glad."

"Me too."

Making the coffees for Richard and his coworker was too routine to keep her mind busy. Taryn found herself wondering how she should behave with Caleb when his sister-in-law was present. She wasn't used to dealing with families, had not gotten that far with any of her last four boyfriends. She finally felt comfortable with Richard's family, but she didn't consider them typical.

When the bell over the door tinkled, she knew without looking that Caleb had arrived. She felt more than saw Emma perk up next to her. Putting the coffees into a to-go carton, she turned around. She felt her smile stretch into a silly grin but couldn't stop it, even if she had wanted to. He was just so damn...*yummy*. She gave Emma a saucy wink as she passed through the counter and headed over to the table Lisa had chosen. Caleb stood next to his sister-in-law, saying something to her though his focus was clearly on Taryn as she approached.

"Ah, my unpaid delivery boy, you're just in time." She handed him the drinks, determined to follow his lead on how he wanted to act in Lisa's presence. She wasn't worried about what her employees or customers would think of her dating two men but she certainly could not assume the same would be true of Caleb and his family, let alone friends and coworkers.

Caleb took the carton and leaned in, kissing her on the lips. It was clearly meant to be a public kiss but her breathing picked up and it took a great deal of willpower not to grab onto him with both hands and sink into the kiss.

"Hi," he whispered against her lips before pulling back.

"Hi." She hoped she didn't sound like an idiot.

"Lisa, this is Taryn. You may have met her. She's been to the bar a few times. Taryn, my sister-in-law Lisa."

Lisa stood to shake hands. "It's nice to see you again. I do remember speaking to you and your...friend about the music one night."

"Yes, Richard and I have enjoyed your place many times but the band was really good that night, your song especially so. I briefly considered doing some live music events here but decided it wasn't the direction I wanted to go."

"Oh, I didn't realize this was your place. It's wonderful. I've just started my daughter Katherine in a school down the street. I got here early for pick-up so thought I'd get a quiet cup of coffee."

"If you ladies don't mind, I've promised to get these coffees across the street while they're still hot. If you're gone before I get back, Lisa, I'll see you for dinner on Sunday. I want to hear all about Katherine's first week at school." He gave Lisa a brief kiss on the cheek then Taryn a not-so-brief kiss on the mouth. She resisted the urge to lick her lips as she watched him walk out the door.

Turning back, she found Lisa watching her. Her stomach churned in nervousness but she fought it down and did her best to keep her smile. "Let me know if there's anything else we can get for you." Knowing she was running away did not stop her from going back behind the counter to ring up the next customer.

She told herself she wasn't paying any more attention than she would to any other customer, but knew that for a lie when her shoulders relaxed as Lisa picked up her purse and headed for the door. Managing a smile when the other woman turned and met her eyes, she gave a cheerful wave goodbye then breathed a sigh of relief.

Checking her watch, she turned to Emma. "Petra and I are having a girl's night tonight. Would you like to come?"

"I would love to, thanks," Emma said with real pleasure in her voice.

Taryn was glad she'd issued the invitation. "Are you good for today, or would you like a couple more hours?"

"I would like lots more hours — I'm saving up for Spring Break — but I have my three o'clock class today. If you can give me until two, though, that would be awesome."

"Perfect. I'm going to see if Caleb has time for lunch, but I can be back by two."

"Caleb, huh?"

"Yes, Caleb Black. Richard and I met him the other night."

"He's frickin' hot."

"Yes. Yes, he is." They giggled together as they watched Caleb come back into the shop. He quirked an eyebrow at their laughter but didn't seem intimidated.

"Do you have time for lunch?" Taryn asked as he approached the counter. "Or would you like a coffee?"

"I would love lunch, if you have time."

Walking to the Mexican restaurant down the street, Taryn smiled and ducked her head when he took her hand in his, swinging their arms like a little kid.

"You make me feel young and alive," he said.

Surprise washed through her, along with a spurt of fear. "That's..." She didn't know how to finish.

Pulling her to a stop, he ran his free hand over her cheek. "That was supposed to make you smile."

She still couldn't smile as she studied his face. "I'm a little bit scared about how...right this is."

"I think you're brave." His voice was low as he studied her face. She wondered what he saw that made his mouth curve up into a smile, made his eyes warm as she watched, made one hand squeeze hers tight while the other caressed her cheek so gently. "Being scared is easy. Doing what needs to be done despite that, that's brave. Everything I learn about you makes me want to learn more." Leaning down, he brushed the barest of kisses across her lips. Pulling in a deep breath, she finally gave him his smile.

"It may be scary, but you're not alone. We're all in this together." Nudging her back into motion, he resumed swinging her hand, smiling when she laughed.

When they were settled, orders placed and guacamole on the table, Taryn felt Caleb's scrutiny like an examination. She darted her eyes to his then blushed at the heat focused on her. She looked away quickly.

"You are so beautiful."

Unable to stop the involuntary jerk of her head, she wasn't the least surprised when he cupped her chin in his hand and forced her to look at him.

His face was hard but compassionate, knowing but implacable.

"Do you think I'm lying to you?"

She blinked, wanting to look away but unable to. "No, I think you're...exaggerating. You haven't known me long enough to think I'm beautiful."

She saw that her answer had surprised him and he released her but she knew he would not let her look away—hide—again.

"You think our perception of beauty changes as we get to know a person?"

"Yes, sometimes. There are plenty of people we simply find attractive, their features somehow coming together in a way that works for many people." He was one such person but she didn't feel the need to point that out.

"Then there are the people we know. Who they are becomes entwined with how we see them, and they're beautiful. Like parents and their children."

"Uh-huh. So you think you're beautiful only to people who know what a good person you are."

"Well...yeah. Basically. Like Richard. He tells me I'm beautiful sometimes, and I believe he sees me that way. But he didn't, not for a long time. Only after he came to love me."

"I can sort of see your logic, so I'm not going to get mad. But let me be real clear here. I'm not in love with you, I've only known you for six days. I think you're beautiful and sexy and I want to get to know you better. Not the other way around, not I've gotten to know you and therefore think you're beautiful. So get used to the idea and don't you dare convince yourself that I'm lying to myself, or you, when I tell you how you look to me. Got it?"

She knew her eyes had grown big as saucers and she couldn't quite speak around the frog in her throat, so she had to swallow a couple of times before she could answer him. "Yes, Caleb."

He leaned in and gave her a quick kiss of approval before returning to the chips and guacamole.

"Taryn."

"Caleb."

"Will you tell me about your family?"

"There's not much to tell. My parents died when I was thirteen. I lived with my grandmother until I was seventeen, but she had to go into a home. I lived with my aunt until I was eighteen. My parents were good parents, they loved me and I miss them still. They left plenty of money so I didn't have to worry about college and I knew that as long as I was careful I'd have enough to buy my own business."

He watched her while she spoke and she had the unnerving sensation that he could see inside her head.

"That's a tough age to lose your parents. How did they die?" He took her hand and brought it to rest on his thigh, his fingers playing with hers.

"They were killed in a train wreck. Their commuter train hit a car that was left on the tracks. Eight people died."

"I'm so sorry. What a tragedy." His warm hand held hers firmly, his thumb rubbing small circles on her wrist.

"It was...horrible. The police and a social worker came to my school to tell me. They took me to my grandmother, but I didn't know her very well. She lived in Arizona."

"So you had to go to a new house, a new school, a new state. You said your parents left money, they didn't leave a guardian?"

"Apparently they had asked a friend, years before, who agreed to be guardian. But when the time came she had moved on, had a husband and kids, a whole different life. When the social workers told her I had a grandmother and an aunt, she figured she was off the hook."

"It never occurred to any of them that if your parents had wanted you to live with your grandmother or your aunt they would have listed them as guardians?"

His voice was eerily calm and she forced a smile to reassure him. "It was fine, we just didn't know each other very well. We pretty much stayed out of each other's way until she became too sick and needed to go into the home. Then I went to Colorado with Aunt Peggy. By then I was seventeen, so we were more like roommates. We didn't bother each other, much."

The food arrived and Taryn was relieved. She didn't like to talk about her teenage years. They sucked, they were over, she had moved on. Caleb was quiet and she was worried what he might be thinking, but when he looked at her she could see only approval and desire on his face.

When they finished, he looked at his watch. "I need to get to an appointment. I have some work to do after but I'm hoping my night will be free. Richard said he would be free tonight, what do you think?"

"I'm having drinks and dinner with my friends Petra and Emma." She watched him, prepared to be pissed if he considered time with her friends less important than time with him. "I wouldn't get there until almost midnight."

"I'd rather have you there sooner, but if later is what I can get, I'll take it." He walked her back to the shop, stopping at the door. He kissed her then, not like earlier, but like that first night. A kiss that went soul deep and left her breathless and hungry for more. "Tonight," he promised, and walked away.

Chapter Six
ℬ

Richard hummed as he prepared dinner. He had been so thrilled to see Caleb that afternoon, even if only for a couple of minutes. They had talked on the phone a number of times but it was shocking how much difference it had made to see him, talk to him, stand next to him. He'd wanted to drag the sexy-as-hell man into his office and attack him.

Grimacing to himself while he chopped the garlic, Richard tried to remember his resolve not to get in too deep. The chances of things working out with both Caleb and Taryn were pretty slim. Probably the two of them would become serious, maybe even marry, leaving Richard on the sidelines. The funny part was, he would be equally jealous of both of them. Where before he had no problem with the idea of Taryn falling in love with someone else and getting married, would have been thrilled for her in fact, now…now things were different. It felt so right, so perfect, when the three of them were together.

He missed Taryn, too. While she rarely spent more than one night at a time with him, they usually got together at least every other day and she generally spent those nights at his place. They hadn't spoken of it but it hadn't felt right for the two of them to get together without Caleb. He was glad that the two had been able to have lunch together and though he wished she was able to make it to dinner, he was pleased at the idea of cooking for Caleb.

Cooking was a valued tradition in his family and he could hold his own with those who made their living at it. It was a skill he was proud of and he liked to show it off. It was a completely different feeling than being a doctor. That was hard work and dedication, not something he was proud of, but something that he felt he had to do.

He moved from the garlic to an onion, chopping while humming to the blues coming from the radio. He wondered what kind of music Caleb liked, what his family was like, what his time in the military had been like. There was so much he wanted to know. Other than Taryn, it had been too long since he was actually interested in a person separate from the sex. He missed that connection, which was probably a big reason why he continued to go back to Taryn. Was he going to be able to handle it if they broke up with him? Would he lose not only the new friend but his best friend as well?

The knock on the door caused his heart to skip a beat. Not wanting to smell of onion, he washed his hands quickly and grabbed a towel to dry them off as he walked to the door. Unlike this afternoon when he had been forced to look at Caleb without touching, the minute he opened the door he grabbed Caleb's hand and pulled him inside, slamming the door shut behind them.

Caleb pushed him against the wall, threading his hands through Richard's hair. Richard felt them clench, pulling his hair tight as Caleb angled him just so and lowered his mouth. Richard was expecting an attack, a harsh reacquainting of lips and tongue. Instead Caleb barely brushed his lips, avoiding Richard's searching advances. The hands in his hair tightened even further and Richard made himself relax, gave himself into the situation. Caleb murmured his appreciation and bit gently at the corner of Richard's mouth then soothed the spot with his tongue.

Somehow Richard found himself relaxed, yet anxious for more. Wanting yet waiting. Breathing deeply but unmoving. Caleb loosened one hand from his hair and moved it down to his neck, his fingers curved around the nape, his thumb on the pulse point in front.

"Caleb." It was a greeting, a plea and a sigh, all at once.

"Richard." It was a promise, a demand and an acknowledgment.

Richard opened his eyes, having no idea when they had closed. Caleb watched him, his thumb moving idly, his eyes fierce. Richard felt his body soften even further, except for that one very hard part of himself. As if that was what he'd been waiting for, Caleb moved in.

Lips met lips, tongue met tongue. Caleb gave and Richard took and they both sighed with pleasure. Then Caleb growled and pushed away, leaving Richard feeling cold and empty.

"We're going to wait. Right, Ricky?"

The tiny hesitation in that last word was enough to remind Richard of where they were and what they were doing. Yes, they should wait. He would feed Caleb dinner, they would talk and then Taryn would come home. He pushed himself off the wall.

"Beer or wine? Something else?" he offered as they walked into the kitchen. He turned at Caleb's growl to find the man staring at his ass. "No," he insisted. "You aren't allowed to be all growly and sexy and expect me to be the stronger person here." He laughed and pushed Caleb to a chair at the table. "Now sit down and behave while I make dinner."

"Yes, Richard."

Richard had to bite his lips to keep from laughing out loud at the strangled resignation in Caleb's voice. He certainly had no doubts about this man wanting him, at least sexually.

He went to the fridge and got them both beers, then returned to the cutting board.

"So, you're in security?" Richard asked.

"That's right. Mostly corporate, but I do some home security as well."

"My sister Laura is a police officer here." He moved to the stove and began to sauté.

"Officer Daniels, of course. I should have noticed the resemblance when I saw your name."

"Well," Richard laughed, "I like to think you were otherwise distracted at the time."

"I certainly was. I've met Laura a few times, I like her. You must be pretty close in age."

"Twins, actually."

"Do you have other siblings? Someone must have gone into the family business—your cooking smells too good for it not to continue on after your parents."

"One brother and one other sister. My sister Michelle is in Italy studying cooking and my brother Brian is finishing his MBA this year. He and my mother get positively giddy discussing the management of the restaurant. I think they want to expand the bar area, give your brother a run for his money."

"I can't believe I've never eaten at Mama's. I tend to find a couple of good restaurants I like and stick with them."

"We'll all go for dinner soon. I'd like you to meet everyone." Richard's eyes widened as he realized what he'd just said. Caleb didn't comment, just watched as Richard plated up the food and brought it to the table.

"It looks delicious. I can't wait."

Richard told Caleb stories about his family, his childhood. There had been plenty of fun and mischief in the Daniels household. He had worked in the restaurant off and on, both in the kitchen and out, until graduating college.

"Why did you decide to become a doctor?" Caleb was pushing his plate away, every bite gone. "That was fantastic."

Richard rose and took their dishes to the kitchen. Caleb followed with more items and began helping to put the food away and the dishes in the dishwasher, both of them taking frequent opportunities to brush against each other.

"When I was seven I was at the restaurant, sitting at a table with my brother and sisters, entertaining ourselves. A man at the table next to us had a heart attack. Luckily there was a doctor eating dinner, too, and she saved the man's life, doing CPR until the ambulance arrived. We were all just stunned, sitting there watching, while this woman, this unassuming woman, was saving a man's life. It stuck with me. I knew I didn't want to go into the restaurant business, I enjoyed it too much as a hobby to risk hating it as a job."

"How did you end up going to college in California?" Caleb asked while they picked out a DVD and settled on the couch.

"I wanted to leave the state. I love my family, but being one of four, and a twin no less, I thought I needed a chance to settle my identity by myself. At least for a while. My dad's sister and her family lived in southern California, so my parents were more comfortable with me going there than anywhere else out of state. They knew I wanted to come back here for medical school, that it was only four years."

"And then you met Taryn."

Richard smiled. "And then I met Taryn."

"Part of me is amazed that you didn't just snatch her up right then and there."

Cocking his head, Richard thought about that while trying to ignore the thigh pressed hard against his, the fingers idly brushing over his knee. "I think that mostly had to do with the fact that while I was comfortably gay while living here, there weren't a lot of options open to me at the time. So when I got to college and there were gay groups on campus, gay bars nearby, I went into a bit of overload. Plus, I was so gung-ho about being gay, determined to be myself and not hide, it took me awhile to realize I was still attracted to women occasionally. It wasn't until I got a crush on my biology teacher that I realized there was no good reason to limit myself just because I found guys attractive more often.

"What about you, Caleb? How come you joined the military?" Richard put his arm on the back of the couch, letting his hand fall to rest on Caleb's shoulder, trying not to let the feel of solid muscles distract him from what the man was saying.

"When I was in college one of my instructors was ex-Navy SEAL. I don't know, I was just so impressed by how intelligent he was, how...steady. I had this vision of military guys as being either dumb grunts or adrenaline junkies. I had a lot of energy and no direction. My parents had money but I wanted to make my own way. I wanted to go new places, see new things and he showed me how."

"You enjoyed it."

"Yes, for the most part. It's a weird thing, the military. It's obviously not just a job, but I didn't want it to be my whole life, either. I didn't want a military family, someone at home waiting for me, wondering if I was going to make it back this time, kids who hated me for dragging them around. Some of my teammates were getting married and getting out and the opportunity came up to start something new with one of them, my partner, Michael. It was something I could be proud of but could also share with my wife and children when the time came, seemed too good to pass up."

"Have you regretted leaving?"

"No. Sometimes I miss the action—that adrenaline rush is addictive for a reason. But I've enjoyed the challenge of building our business and I like knowing that when the time comes I'll be able to have a family without worrying about leaving them behind."

"You're a good guy, Caleb Black." The hand on his knee squeezed briefly.

"You're not so bad yourself, Dr. Daniels."

"Have you, uh..." Richard didn't know what had possessed him to start the sentence, but he was determined to finish it. "Have you done the sex clubs and stuff?"

"And stuff?"

Richard scoffed. "You know what I mean."

"I do, and I'm sorry, I don't mean to make fun. I want you to be able to ask me this kind of thing. To answer your question, yes, I did go through a club phase, learning to what extent I wanted to take the whole Dominance and submission thing."

"And?" Richard hoped he managed to keep his voice even, because he thought the answer to this question was going to be very important to him.

"And I found that while the clubs were fascinating and I enjoyed my time there, I wasn't interested in playing with strangers, or in having a slave."

"So the other night was fairly typical?"

"No, the other night was...special. But if you mean did I hold back what I wanted, then no. I got what I wanted. I imagine, if things continue on like I hope they will, that sometimes we'll do more than we did the other night, and sometimes less. I don't need a scene every time I have sex, but I will push for certain things when I want them and feel you're both ready and willing."

"But you're not going to try to talk us into going to a club or sharing us with strangers."

"Hell no." Caleb's voice was steel and left no doubt.

"Okay, cool. Just checking."

"Good. Now turn on the movie before I forget we're waiting for Taryn to get here."

Richard smiled and turned on the movie.

* * * * *

Caleb looked up at Taryn when she walked into the living room. He'd heard her at the door and would have gone to let her in but hadn't wanted to disturb Richard. Sprawled on the wide, comfortable couch, with Richard's head on his chest, he was watching the end of the movie, waiting for her. His fingers were tangled in Richard's hair, stroking the sleeping man. He watched Taryn's reaction, not surprised to see her licking her lips. He wanted to see if he could get her to bite her lower lip, even though it wasn't much of a challenge.

"I told him to take a nap since we had plans to keep him up half the night," he said quietly. And yep, there it went, plump lip being nibbled on by small, white teeth. *Tasty.* "Come here."

She walked to him slowly, kneeling down beside the couch.

"Closer."

She leaned in, stopping just short of his lips. He growled and watched the pleased smile stretch across her face.

"Oh, it's like that is it?"

Her smile blossomed into a full grin. "Too bad you can't reach me, isn't it?"

"Taryn."

"Caleb."

"Put your lips on mine."

She gave him a saucy grin then did as she was told. He drank her in, only her lips touching him while his arms were full of Richard. Not bad. For a start. He drew back. "Maybe you should wake Sleeping Beauty."

Sighing happily, she complied. Caleb watched her lay her lips lightly on his lover's. She knew those lips better than he did. She knew his body, his heart. But he would learn. He had to, because he wasn't letting them go, either of them.

Richard's body stirred, his lips parting under Taryn's delicate touch. She took full advantage and surged in, wringing a groan from Richard who started to bring his hands up to hold her to him. Caleb used his arm to hold Richard's in place and felt Richard shiver in response. He saw Taryn's hands move toward Richard, saw the moment she realized that would change the game and rested them on the couch instead. He smiled. They were perfect, so perfect. He didn't know what he'd done to deserve them, but he was thankful for it.

While Richard and Taryn touched only at the mouth, Caleb began to use his hands. He pressed firmly on Richard's arm, signaling that it stay in place. He moved one hand up to Taryn's nape and the other began a slow slide under the hem of Richard's t-shirt and along the waistband of his shorts. At Taryn's neck, his thumb brushed over her jawline and up to their joined lips. They broke apart and Richard bit Caleb's thumb.

"Let's go into the bedroom," he growled.

They stumbled to the bed, legs and arms entwined. Caleb briefly considered stepping back, regaining control and slowing things down, but it had been so long, too long. There was no way he could take the time to torment them with foreplay, it would be too much torture for him. They tried to tear each other's clothes off but got tangled up. It didn't even slow them down. Richard and Caleb kissed, Taryn wrapped a hand around both cocks. Caleb still wore his shirt, Richard's pants were caught at his knees and Taryn's bra dangled from one arm. They twisted and turned until they managed to get on the bed.

Caleb barely remembered to grab a condom and put one on while Taryn shoved Richard down and covered his cock with her mouth. Richard clenched his fists in the spread, whipping his head from side to side. Caleb reached for Taryn, testing her, so thankful to find her soaked. He was going too fast, showing no finesse, but they were right there with him, desperate to be inside each other. Too long, it had been too long.

Taryn hummed and Richard groaned. Caleb grabbed her hips and eased himself slowly inside her, determined not to rush this one thing. She squeezed so tight around him that he had to pause and wait for her to open to him. Heaven, pure heaven.

"Baby, you feel so good." He leaned down to kiss her shoulder, inhaling the combined scents of Taryn and Richard.

"Oh yeah, you feel soooo good," Richard agreed.

Taryn took her mouth from Richard.

"Caleb," she begged, spurring him to action. Richard erupted and Caleb watched Taryn drink him down. He felt her flutter then spasm as she collapsed on top of Richard, spent. He reached down and picked her up so that she was on her knees, back to his chest. His eyes were on Richard who took the hint, scooting forward so that he could play with her clit.

He saw Taryn look down just as Richard's tongue touched both her slit and Caleb's cock, heard her breath catch. Richard helped him support Taryn so that he could move in and out of her. His strokes became shorter, more desperate, and he reached around to brush her nipples before clamping down on them with his fingers. She screamed and came again. He let himself go, holding her up as she nearly collapsed. Richard helped ease them down and they somehow managed to get under the covers.

Caleb woke sometime later to find himself spooned around Richard who was in turn spooned around Taryn. He supposed that made the most sense, height wise. He couldn't resist, even knowing poor Richard had to go to work in a couple of hours. He began nibbling an earlobe while his hand crept between Taryn's legs. He played with her curls and wondered if she would like being shaved. They might have to try it sometime.

Sucking Richard's earlobe between his teeth, he gave it a sharp nip. The other man's rear pressed more fully into his cock, which was already hard. Taryn was still motionless though becoming wet, so he whispered in Richard's ear.

"Let's show her what two mouths can do."

"Mmmm."

Caleb got out of bed and walked around to the other side, getting two condoms out and handing one to Richard. They put them on then arranged themselves next to the still-sleeping Taryn. Eyes on each other, they synchronized their movements. Each cupped a breast, shaped it, tested it, then lowered a mouth to the tip.

Taryn made a noise that was half moan, half squeak. Caleb's eyes were glued to Richard who followed his every movement. They pulled her nipples up, letting them loose with a plop, then turned to look at her. There were tears falling from her eyes and Caleb's heart stuttered in alarm.

"Baby, what's wrong?" He sounded desperate, even to his own ears.

"Sweetie, what—?" Richard asked, adding to Caleb's certainty that Taryn wasn't usually a crier.

She shook her head. "Nothing, you're just so beautiful, the two of you. You make me feel so good."

Without even looking at each other, both men rose to nuzzle the wet tracks from her face.

"No more of that now. You're going to scare me and I'm supposed to be fearless."

She gave him a tremulous smile and leaned up to kiss him. He gave in readily, soothing her and himself with her sweetness. He felt, more than saw, Richard move down between her legs. He used his hands to please her abandoned breasts, all the while keeping their kiss going. They stayed that way for what seemed like forever before Taryn could no longer contain her need.

"Please, Caleb. Please."

Caleb moved down to give each nipple a farewell kiss then scooted back. Richard had risen to kneel between her legs, his lips shiny from her cream. Caleb reached over to guide him to her entrance, letting just the head slide in before he squeezed the shaft.

"Don't move." His command was whispered but Richard grunted his anguished acknowledgment.

Caleb knelt behind Richard and lubed his ass until he saw Richard's arms shaking with strain and need. Then he pushed into him, slowly, as he'd done with Taryn earlier.

"Caleb...I can't...please."

"Give it to her, Ricky, take her." And as Richard surged into Taryn, Caleb seated himself fully inside Richard. Richard waited until Caleb began to move, then matched his strokes. They moved as if choreographed, drawing it out, until they could no longer be slow. Caleb began pounding into Richard who let his movements fuck Taryn as well. Caleb wasn't sure who came first, only that they all screamed in completion before once again collapsing to the bed.

* * * * *

Caleb and Taryn had to bribe Richard with coffee to get him out of bed the next morning. Neither of them had to be anywhere for hours but Richard had appointments starting at nine. They dragged him to the kitchen table and left him to drink coffee while they made breakfast.

They were comfortable together, anticipating each other's moves and needs. Things were moving fast but Caleb already felt like he was a part of their lives, and they were part of his. Walking into the coffee shop yesterday, knowing that Lisa was inside, had been slightly unnerving. High-school prom was the last time he had brought a date home and it had been strange introducing Taryn to his sister-in-law. Not bad, just strange. On the one hand, he wanted Taryn to like his family. On the other hand, he didn't have any plans to stop seeing her, or Richard, if his family didn't like or approve of them.

That was what felt so strange, he realized. The idea that he was seeking anyone's approval to make a place for these two people in his life. Because he didn't want them to be a small part, kept away from the rest of his life. It was already clear to him that they needed to be integral and that meant making them comfortable with his friends and family.

When Richard left the table to go take his shower, Caleb had to restrain himself from joining in and making the poor man late for work. He eyed Taryn, then the kitchen table they'd broken in last week. She saw him looking and smirked at him.

"You don't work office hours?" she asked.

"Sometimes. I make a lot of the onsite visits. Meeting clients at their offices to do the initial consult, following up on problem incidents. I'm not fond of staying in one seat all day."

"Neither am I. If I have to be at my computer for more than an hour, I get jittery. Even at home, I hardly use it."

Richard came out shortly, dressed for work. He gave them both a quick kiss, then strode out the door. Caleb had a vision of them like this, ten years in the future. It wasn't quite the future he would have guessed at two weeks ago, but suddenly it was the one he wanted more than anything he could remember in a very long time.

The look on Taryn's face suggested she might be thinking something very similar, but the crinkle between her brows warned him he needed to stay on his toes. Everything was falling into place so easily, it was only a matter of time before reality hit. He hoped he was ready for it. He hoped *they* were ready for it because no matter the difficulties, he had every intention of seeing his vision come true.

Chapter Seven

ဢ

Three weeks later, Taryn turned the "Closed" sign on the door of Grounded then leaned her forehead against it. It had been a long day. Early in the morning a man had come in who had, for some reason, made her uncomfortable. Something about the way he sat watching everything going on around him unnerved her. He sipped one coffee after another for long enough that Taryn seriously considered calling Caleb and asking him to stop by and tell her she was being paranoid. She hadn't wanted to leave the shop while the man was there and so had skipped lunch, settling for a pastry. He finally left shortly after the lunch crowd thinned out.

Later, one of her employees, Stan, had spilled hot coffee on himself and she had taken him across the street to the medical building. By the time she got back to the shop her two remaining employees were in over their heads. She had grabbed Caleb the minute he walked in the door a short while later, barely giving him a kiss before she shoved him behind the counter to help.

Turning around, still leaning against the door, she gave him a weary smile. "Sorry about that."

Taking off the apron he'd worn to protect his suit, he came to her. Cupping her face in his hands, he leaned in and kissed her gently on her mouth, her eyes, her nose. "You've had a tough day. I'm glad I could help a little. The tips were nice, but I think I'll keep my day job."

She smiled. "That's okay, I'm pretty sure I couldn't afford you. In fact, I just don't know how I'm going to be able to pay you for your help today." She pushed her hips forward, meeting the length of him. Moisture pooled between her legs at the hard contact.

His grin was feral. "I'm sure we can work something out."

He kissed her, long and slow, until she was melting against his body. When he pulled away, she whimpered. Opening her eyes, she found him watching her, his look at once hungry and possessive, but also soft and slightly awed. Her heart stuttered.

Steadying her with his large hands on her shoulders, Caleb took a step back, narrowing his eyes at her when she moved her lips into a pout.

"I spoke to Richard a few minutes ago. He's making us a very late dinner at my house, since we all have tomorrow off. And you've got two employees still here, trying to close up."

Taryn's stomach growled at the thought of an actual meal. The two pastries she had scarfed down were not cutting it. She began running through the final closing steps for the shop. She and her employees had done as much of the cleanup as possible in the last half hour as things had finally slowed down. Now Derek was cleaning up the coffee machines while Sara worked in the kitchen.

"Did you stop by for anything in particular?" she asked as she mopped the floor. He moved ahead of her, putting the chairs up on the tables.

"I had a late meeting with my brother so I thought I'd stop by for coffee and a kiss." He grinned at her. "I didn't know you'd put me to work."

They finished up quickly and she locked the door and said goodbye to her employees.

Getting into his SUV and closing her eyes, Taryn let the stresses of the day fall away. The trip to Caleb's house took only ten minutes, but she fell asleep, waking when Caleb opened her door and reached over her to unlock the seatbelt.

When they walked into the house, the delicious aromas of dinner greeted them, along with a kiss for each from Richard.

"I put the pasta in when I heard you pull up. It will be ready in a second."

Taryn's stomach rumbled as she went to wash her hands. When she came back out she saw that the table was set, and Caleb was lighting the candles while Richard put the food out.

Her heart gave a quick squeeze of love at the sight of her two men. She had loved Richard for a long time, but had known something was lacking in their relationship. They had been better off as friends, lovers even, but not truly a couple. Until they met Caleb. Where they hadn't been a couple, only two individuals who cared deeply for each other, with Caleb they were more, the three of them were a unit.

Remembering how she had worried that starting something with Caleb would threaten the relationship she had with Richard, she marveled that instead it had been strengthened. He added so much more, she couldn't imagine not having him with them anymore.

They ate the delicious meal, then worked together to clean it up.

"I'm so ready for a day off tomorrow," Taryn said as they moved into the living room. "I sincerely hope nobody calls in with any coffee emergencies." She flopped onto the couch and leaned her head back, closing her eyes.

"Not only do I not have to go in, I'm not even on call." Richard joined her on the couch then laid his head on her lap. She ran her fingers through his hair.

Caleb sat on the coffee table and looked at them. Taryn's breathing picked up when she saw the look on his face, and she heard Richard's do the same. Taryn had learned over the past three weeks that while Caleb liked to be in charge in the bedroom, he didn't find it necessary to make every sexual encounter a game of dominance. Many nights she was happy to have sweet sex with her men. It never failed, however, when

Caleb gave that certain look, used that certain voice, or took her with just that kiss, that her body became eager for his mastery.

"Do you trust me?"

Neither Taryn nor Richard hesitated even a moment.

"Yes, Caleb," they answered in unison.

He stood and they did as well. "I've been shopping. Get ready and I'll meet you in the bedroom."

Taryn went to the guest bathroom, wondering what Caleb had bought. All this time he had made use of whatever was handy to pleasure them, or what toys they already had. He had restrained her with silk ties once, bathrobe ties another time. Her favorite was when he had Richard do the restraining for him. She shivered in anticipation. Sometimes he preferred making them obey him without benefit of restraints. He had used the few toys she owned — her silicone vibrator, the little finger vibrator she'd bought for the bathtub, and the vibrating egg. Before, she had only ever used her toys when alone. He added them into their group play with amazing results.

Excited, she went into the master bedroom and sat on the side of the bed next to Richard, waiting. She heard the sink in the bathroom shut off, then Caleb came in. He looked so sexy. He had changed into a pair of worn jeans and wore nothing else. He was well aware that both she and Richard found this to be his most appealing look. As hot as he looked naked, or in a suit, to them nothing compared to the worn-out jeans with nothing else.

"I want you both naked."

Taryn stood up slowly, as did Richard. She pulled her shirt over her head then reached down to remove her socks. Unbuttoning her jeans, she slid them down, her eyes glued to Caleb's, which were hot as he watched them both. When they were naked, they stood waiting.

"I am a lucky bastard."

Taryn blushed when he said it, then moaned when he kissed her. He dominated the kiss, giving her a taste of what was to come. Sliding one hand up to cup the back of her neck, he broke the kiss then used the hand that he had similarly on Richard's nape to bring the other man to him for a kiss. All three were breathing hard when he pulled back.

Caleb reached down into a drawer and pulled out a handful of leather cuffs. Holding four in each hand, he extended one set to each of them. "Do you trust me?" he asked again.

They answered by immediately reaching out and accepting his offerings. Taryn had learned in the past weeks that if she did what Caleb told her to do, the pleasure would be exquisite. He had never done anything to give her the slightest pause or doubt. He had taught her things about her body, as well as his and Richard's. She trusted him completely.

"Do your ankles first, then you can help each other with the wrists." They did as they were told then stood still while Caleb checked each cuff to make sure that they weren't too tight. Satisfied, he returned to the drawer. Taryn shivered. He had restrained them before, but there was something different about wearing a cuff meant solely for this purpose. She flexed her fingers, amazed at how different it was to put them on like this, rather than have Caleb restrain her when she was already mindless with lust.

Caleb went to Richard and kissed him. As his tongue plundered Richard's mouth, his hands ran down the man's shoulders to his wrists and brought them gently behind his back. Richard's heavy breathing hitched as Caleb used a metal clasp to attach the two wrist cuffs together. Taryn sucked her lower lip between her teeth. She watched as Richard's cock grew harder, a small drop beading at the head.

Her eyes moved to Caleb as he came to her. Leaning down, he took first one breast, then the other, into his mouth, as much as he could. Pulling back, he moved to kiss her neck, then the curve of her shoulder as his hands tenderly drew her arms behind her and attached the cuffs together.

"Go stand at the foot of the bed, one on each post." He turned his back to rifle through the drawer again as they followed his instructions.

The bed was a giant four poster with sturdy wood posts. Taking more cuffs from the drawer, Caleb wrapped them around the bed posts then attached them to the clips holding their wrists together. The contours of the posts were such that the cuff would not be able to move up or down more than half an inch.

Though she had been expecting it and had experienced similar, the actuality of being cuffed by him, bound to an immovable object, had her eyes wide, her breath fast and cream dripping down her thighs. He had positioned them so that they were facing in toward each other as much as possible. Taryn looked at Richard, saw the same trepidation and arousal on his face and wished that she could touch him.

Caleb knelt at Richard's feet and pulled a bar from beneath the bed. He attached it to the ankle cuffs, spreading Richard's legs so that he couldn't move them. Then he quickly did the same with Taryn. When he was finished he stood in front of them, the apex of the triangle they formed together. He looked at them carefully, reached one hand to cup Taryn's sopping pussy, and used his thumb to move the moisture Richard had produced around the head of his penis.

Stepping back, he looked at them. She absorbed the hot look in his eyes like a shot of whiskey. The fact that seeing them like this, standing at the ready for him, gave him such pleasure, satisfied her like no alcohol could.

He returned to the drawer and came back with something small enough to fit in his fist. Taryn looked down into the hand he held in front of her and gasped. Nipple clamps. She had never tried them, associated them with painful bondage. She said nothing but took a deep breath and consciously relaxed her shoulders.

Caleb stepped in close to her. He dropped the clamps onto the bed and cupped her breasts in his hands. He had bound her wrists just above the small of her back, so her breasts were lifted out as offerings to him. He took them, caressed them lightly at first, then, in tandem, pinched the nipples hard. She gasped again, this time in total pleasure, no fear, feeling the answering tug in her vagina.

She moaned when he took one nipple into his mouth, sucking hard on it then flicking at it with his tongue. She whimpered when he pulled back then watched wide-eyed as he took up a clamp and brought it to her wet nipple. The clamp went easily on her hardened peak. There was a little pain but Taryn felt more cream slide down her leg at the sensation.

"Caleb!"

"One more. You can do it, baby, I know you'll like it." He picked up the other clamp as he worshiped her free breast with his mouth. He pulled the nipple between his teeth and tugged hard then released it. He put the other clamp on then blew air on both dark red nipples. Taryn gasped again. He kissed her then moved away.

Taryn was bereft until she opened her eyes and saw him sucking on Richard's nipple. Richard had thrown his head back and didn't see when Caleb brought the clamp up to the first nipple and attached it. He gave a small bellow and his eyes popped open wide. He was breathing so hard, Caleb had to time the second clamp just so. When he had it placed, he gripped Richard's cock tightly, his thumb brushing over the head until Richard strained against his bonds.

Again, Caleb stepped back to survey his lovers. Clearly pleased with what he saw, he nodded his approval. Going back to the drawer, he pulled out a butt plug and bottle of lube. He stood behind Richard and prepared the plug with a generous amount of lube.

"Are you ready for me?" he murmured.

"Always," Richard gasped as Caleb pressed on his shoulder, forcing him to bend, despite the awkwardness on his bound arms. Taryn couldn't see Caleb's hands but knew the instant he thrust the plug home by Richard's grunt and the sweat dotting his brow. Caleb's hand on Richard's shoulder pulled him back, while the other hand snaked around his hip to play with his hard cock.

Taryn saw Caleb bite Richard's shoulder before he pulled away and returned to the drawer. She swallowed hard when she saw another, smaller plug. Caleb had used his finger in her, as had Richard, but they hadn't put anything else into her yet. She wanted to reach the point where they could both fill her up, but wasn't sure she was ready. If Caleb thought she was ready for this, though, she would trust him. He stepped forward and laid the lube and the plug on the bed, along with a small dildo she hadn't seen him take out. As he did so he thumbed a remote he was holding and she heard Richard give a surprised start.

Caleb moved to kneel in front of Richard and buckled a cock strap around him. Rising, he used his hands to come all the way up Richard's body then gently tweaked the nipple clamps.

"Ah fuck!"

"Eventually."

Taryn was not so distracted by the sight of Richard's straining that she didn't see Caleb pick up the bottle of lube, open it and tuck it into his pocket. He picked up the small plug and the dildo before coming to straddle her leg. He looked hard at both of them.

"Do not come unless I say you can."

He slid the silicone cock into her wetness in one smooth thrust. She worked hard not to move while Caleb slid it in and out of her. Keeping her eyes glued to the sexy vision in front of her, Taryn concentrated on watching the sweat roll down Richard's chest. She saw him jerk forward as he watched Caleb work the dildo in and out. Fighting to stay still, knowing she wasn't supposed to rock forward into his hand, was supremely difficult but she managed it. She was rewarded with a kiss to her shoulder. With his free hand he brought a very slick finger to her rear hole and rubbed it back and forth.

Taryn's butt clenched, holding his finger immobile before she relaxed. He tickled her and she couldn't keep from moving forward, then back. As she moved back he pushed the finger all the way in. Taryn moaned. Caleb added a second finger, scissoring them apart, stretching her. She looked at Richard again and saw that he was straining forward, against his bonds. Caleb saw as well.

"Richard," he barked.

Richard's glazed eyes met his, then he blinked. He relaxed back, his shoulders quivering.

Caleb picked up the plug and lubed it liberally. He laid it against her hole and gently pushed. She took a deep breath and bore down on it. The tip slipped inside and Caleb paused, letting her adjust. The feeling was very different from his fingers, as she tightened around it. Her muscles clenched, squeezing both objects inside her.

"Caleb, please." He went back to working the fake cock in and out of her pussy with one hand and when she breathed in, urged the plug the rest of the way inside her with the other. Stepping in front of her now that the plug was seated, Caleb worked the dildo in and out, twisting it around. Her passage was tight, filled as she was. He seated it fully then reached up and took off the nipple clamps.

Taryn wailed as sensation rushed back into her nipples. Caleb moved the toy in and out of her. Her fingers were clenching, unable to grasp anything, unable to move, do anything but stand there and take what he gave her.

"Caleb, I need...please...Caleb."

"Come now." He leaned in and took a nipple into his mouth and she erupted. The spasms went on and on. Her knees went weak and Caleb supported her with his arm. He waited until she was almost done then dropped to his knees, removed the dildo and plunged his tongue into her.

It took both of his hands to hold her up now. She went over again, fast and hard, her vision graying, her breath rasping. She didn't have enough energy to scream this time. Caleb licked her clean, then, supporting her with his body, released her from the spreader bar, then the bedpost. He settled her onto the floor and reattached the cuff to the bed at a comfortable spot. Taryn was surprised—he had never kept them bound for very long in one night, but she was too worn out to care. She rolled her head to look at Richard.

Richard's cock was dark and wet, his breathing fast. Caleb placed a kiss on Taryn's forehead then went to Richard. Taryn watched him attack Richard's mouth with his own, then watched his hands sneak up to the clamped nipples. He removed the clips simultaneously then dropped to his knees and enveloped the straining erection in his mouth. He reached to the bed and took the remote in one hand while the other came around to release the cock strap.

Richard tensed visibly when it was removed, clearly fighting his release. Caleb took his mouth off him, turned up the dial on the remote and said, "Now." He covered the shaft with his mouth as Richard bellowed with his eruption. Caleb released his ankles while licking Richard's dick clean. He came up to release him from the bedpost, then lowered him to the floor, reattaching him at a comfortable level, as he had done with Taryn.

Caleb returned from the bathroom with a couple of warm washcloths. Richard watched him use one on Taryn's backside. His cock jerked at the thought of Caleb and him taking her at the same time, and he wished he could stroke it. Probably it was for the best that his hands were otherwise occupied. He might not have been able to resist the need otherwise.

These last few weeks had been amazing. He had never felt such a strong connection to a man so quickly as he did with Caleb, and it was amazing how much it had deepened his relationship with Taryn. The group they formed together was so much more than he could imagine with either alone. He had always loved Taryn, but now was *in love* with her. And Caleb. At the same time. He was afraid to tell either of them, not sure what exactly the future was for them. He only knew that he was happier with the two of them than he had ever been in a relationship.

Caleb used the other cloth on Taryn's front then went back to the bathroom. When he came back he used fresh cloths on Richard. Richard arched his back to push farther into Caleb's grip, the washcloth on his still-sensitive cock almost too much. It had been an incredible climax. He loved it when Caleb took him into his mouth—there was no other feeling like it. Not to say that he didn't love it when Taryn took him also. It was different. They just felt totally different.

Caleb dropped the washcloth and retrieved two pillows from the bed. He placed one in front of Richard.

"On your knees now." Caleb leaned over Richard to once again adjust the strap holding him to the bedpost. Richard had to swallow hard to keep in a groan. He could hardly wait to see what else Caleb had planned. He rose to his knees and licked the hip bone that was conveniently in front of his face, while pulling the pillow under him. Caleb leaned his body into him further while he made the adjustments.

"Okay?" Caleb asked softly, running his hand over Richard's chest and up his neck.

"Very okay." He looked into Caleb's eyes, hoping to show him his love, even though he wasn't ready to give him the words. Caleb blinked then leaned in slowly, never losing eye contact, to give him a soft kiss.

"Good."

Richard tried to ignore his slowly swelling cock while he watched Caleb help Taryn into the same position. She looked so beautiful. Flushed and sated, but starting to get aroused again. Her nipples were still red from the clamps, still peaked. She leaned her head against Caleb's thigh as he made the adjustments behind her then helped her get the pillow under her knees.

When he was finished, Caleb stood in front of them and removed his jeans. His cock sprang free, hard and ready, and Richard licked his lips. Caleb came to Richard and fed him just the tip. Richard knew that Caleb would remember his gag reflex, so he didn't worry about Caleb giving him too much. His throat spasmed at the idea of feeling that thick cock as far as it could go. He sucked hard on the head then licked all around it, playing with the slit. Caleb groaned then backed away.

He moved to Taryn who eagerly opened her mouth and slid down, nearly to the root. Richard was amazed she could take so much, though she had practiced on him often enough. He watched as Caleb held steady, letting Taryn decide how far she could go, her head setting the pace. Licking his lips, Richard hoped Caleb would come back for more on his side. It had been a while since he'd experimented, and with Caleb he wanted to try, see how much of him he could take in.

When Caleb backed away from Taryn, he bent down to give her a kiss before turning back to Richard. Richard opened his mouth readily. Too enthusiastic in his excitement, he dropped his head too far over Caleb's erection and immediately gagged. Caleb pulled back and put his hand on Richard's head, stroking his hair while Richard fought to relax his throat.

"Easy now," Caleb said, softly. "Take it easy."

Richard's shoulders slumped and he refused to look up at Caleb.

Caleb dropped to his knees, the hand in his hair lifting Richard's face to meet his straight on.

Lust still burned in Caleb's eyes, but it was tempered by compassion.

He smashed their lips together, a fierce taking leaving Richard with no questions as to how much the man desired him. Abruptly Caleb pulled back, gave him a stern look and stood back up, bringing his cock right back to Richard's eye level.

"Lick it."

Richard wet his lips and did as he was told. He licked from the root to the head, then back down again. He swirled his tongue around then took the head in his mouth again and sucked hard, before licking down the side. Caleb's hands tightened in his hair as he let out a groan, spurring Richard on. He wanted to make this man come down his throat. He used his teeth to nibble a bit and Caleb's shaft jerked.

Caleb stepped back and Richard lunged forward, caught by his wrists. Caleb gently pushed him back then leaned down and kissed him, before going back to Taryn. Richard was breathing hard again, his cock straining for contact. He wished he could join them, wished he could use his tongue on Taryn's pussy while she sucked Caleb. She moaned and Caleb's back arched as he came. Taryn swallowed but it overwhelmed her mouth. Caleb staggered back to Richard and presented him with his cream-coated cock. Richard leaned in and cleaned him up, the salty taste just what he needed.

Caleb unlatched all of the cuffs and they staggered onto the bed. Caleb sat against the headboard and pulled Taryn into his lap. She rested her head against his shoulder but her eyes were glued to Richard's growing erection.

"Taryn."

"Yes, Caleb."

"Are you wet?"

"Y-yes."

"Show Richard. Let me taste."

Taryn used her hands to open her lips to Richard's view. He sat cross-legged a foot in front of her and could easily see the moisture gathered there.

"She's gorgeous and juicy."

Taryn used two fingers to wipe up some of her cream then offered them over her shoulder to Caleb. He took the fingers in his mouth and sucked them clean. Richard had to keep his hands fisted on his thighs so he wouldn't touch anything without permission.

"Richard, touch yourself, but don't come."

Richard did as he was told and watched Caleb's fingers come around to Taryn's glistening folds and start playing with her. Richard began by matching his strokes with Caleb's, but it became too much. He had to slow down or he was going to come, and he was really hoping Caleb would let him come inside Taryn. Caleb moved his wet fingers to Taryn's clit and squeezed. She jerked and moaned, her hands resting on his knees beside her.

"Taryn, lie down." When she got up, Richard was amazed to see Caleb was already hard again. Taryn lay down between them, the cuffs on her wrists and ankles dark against her pale skin, a turn-on Richard had never expected.

Caleb reached over and got two condoms. He handed one to Richard and put one on himself. He gestured to the lube on the bed behind Richard. Richard grabbed the bottle and opened it, preparing to squeeze it over Caleb's cock. Caleb took the bottle from him though, and used it on Richard's straining penis.

Richard's eyes went wide as he glanced from Caleb to Taryn. Caleb's hands felt amazing on him, squeezing him firmly, but not as amazing as pushing himself into someone's tight hole was going to feel. He didn't think Taryn was ready though.

Caleb handed him back the bottle then moved up over Taryn, entering her in one smooth thrust.

"Caleb!"

Caleb leaned down and kissed her, then flattened himself on her, resting his forearms on either side to make sure he didn't give her too much weight. Her arms came around him, trying to get him closer.

"Richard."

"Y-yes, Caleb."

"Start with your fingers."

Spurred into action, Richard put lube on his fingers. He carefully tickled one wet finger over the larger man's hole, watching it flutter. Caleb moved his mouth to Taryn's and Richard pushed one finger in. Caleb's asshole seemed to suck him in eagerly so he added another finger.

Caleb groaned and Taryn whimpered. Richard moved the fingers in and out until they were sliding smoothly, then added another.

"Hurry, please," Taryn begged.

Making sure his cock was slick, Richard brought it to the waiting pucker. He braced his hands on Caleb's hips and moved in gently. Caleb thrust his ass back, impaling himself on Richard. Then he moved forward, pounding back into Taryn. Richard picked up his rhythm and they fucked in tandem. Taryn reached her legs up, sliding them behind Richard's ass. Her hands were in Caleb's hair, pulling him in closer.

"Hell, oh hell. Caleb..." Richard panted, wishing he could last longer. But there was no way, not the first time he got to fill this tight hole.

Caleb reached one hand to Taryn's clit and sucked her still sensitive nipples. She bucked and screamed.

"You're both so fucking perfect. I love you. Now, come now."

They all erupted together, collapsing in a messy pile. Richard carefully pulled out and removed his condom. Caleb was still lying with his eyes closed, so Richard removed his condom, too, and went to the bathroom to dispose of them and get a couple of washcloths. Now he knew why the man had so many of the things.

Caleb grunted his thanks and used one cloth on Taryn while she and Richard used one on Caleb. They threw the cloths back toward the bathroom and got under the covers. Richard rested his head on Caleb's shoulder, his arm wrapped halfway around Taryn who was lying partly on Caleb.

Richard looked into Taryn's face and they both opened their mouths.

"Love you, too," they said in unison, and both smiled when they felt the arms holding them squeeze tighter.

Chapter Eight

ಎ

Caleb was very much not used to being unsure and it pissed him off that he was very unsure right now. Last night had been everything he had hoped it would be times ten. He had been unable, at the end, to keep from telling them he loved them. That they had responded in kind still made his chest hurt, in a good way.

But...

"Fuck." He dipped his head under the spray of the shower and let the water wash over him. He wanted more. He wanted to come home and know that one or both of them would be there. He wanted to feel free to walk through the door because it was his door, too. He wanted a home. With them. This was new, not something he had ever wanted with anyone before and it left him...unsure.

Disgusted with himself, he pulled his head out of the water and reached for the shampoo. He believed that they loved him. How could that be the easy part? It was everything else that was complicated. Believing Richard loved him did not keep him from being aware that the other man was holding back. Not in bed, not in trust, but despite the love there was something there that Richard was not giving and it was time to find out what that was.

And Taryn. Again, he fully believed she loved him and that she liked him as well, liked spending time with him, with and without Richard, but she was very careful to not spend every night with them. He hadn't really noticed at first, because they all had such different schedules. If she had a late closing it was easier for her just to go home upstairs than to come to his or Richard's house. Or she might be having a girls' night with her friends or babysitting for Petra, her friend from Richard's office. Whatever it was, somehow it ended up that she wasn't with them at least two nights a week.

It wasn't that he minded, exactly. He enjoyed the time spent with Richard, just as he enjoyed the times he was alone with Taryn. Suspecting she was keeping her distance intentionally, however, was another matter. This relationship shit was very annoying. Usually he was in a relationship until it became annoying and then he wasn't. This was annoying but there was no way he wasn't going to do whatever was necessary to fix it. It was...annoying. He sighed and resisted the temptation to bang his head against the shower wall.

Toweling himself off, he checked on Richard. The good doctor was lying diagonally across the bed, head pillowed on one arm while the other was tucked under his cheek. His fabulously naked ass was only half concealed by the sheet. Caleb smiled in satisfaction. Tossing the towel onto the counter, he moved to the bed. Sitting down carefully so as not to jog the bed, he reached one hand out and brushed it lightly across Richard's back, causing a shiver. Caleb moved his hand down to the tempting ass and used a finger to trace the contours, which clenched and unclenched in response.

Richard opened his eyes and rolled over, Caleb letting his finger trail across his lover's butt and over hip as the body moved under him. Caleb studied his face, hoping to find the answers he needed. "I love you, Ricky."

Richard's face, relaxed from sleep, went blank. He closed his eyes. "I love you, too."

"Open your eyes."

Richard shook his head. Caleb's stomach clenched in unfamiliar fear. He forced himself to watch, to observe. Bringing his hand up to settle on Richard's throat in gentle but unmistakable warning, he growled, "Don't lie to me."

Richard forced his eyes open and Caleb saw that they were wet and sad. Part of him wanted to pull the man to him, hug him close and tell him that everything would be all right. Another part of him wanted to pull him over his knee and spank his ass until Richard acknowledged what they had.

Richard kept his eyes on Caleb's. "I love you, too."

Caleb saw the truth, heard it, felt it. But there was still a wariness. Caleb waited. Richard sighed, letting his eyes fall closed again. "It's going to hurt like hell when you leave." There was real pain on his face and in his voice, which was the only thing that kept Caleb from erupting in anger. He very carefully took his hands from Richard and rose from the bed.

He pulled on running clothes and shoes mechanically, all while listening to Richard sit up and pull the sheet and blanket around himself in defense. Caleb refused to look back, just tied his shoes and left before he said something that couldn't be taken back.

Passing the living room, he waved vaguely at Taryn who was curled up on the couch with a book and a bowl of cereal. He opened the door and paused at the idea that he didn't need a key, didn't need to lock up behind him so that he could come back to an empty house. How had he not even been aware that he needed that until he saw it within his grasp? Frustrated with himself, he stretched on the porch then jogged down the front walk.

Abruptly he stopped, stilling as his whole body tuned in to the surroundings, seeking danger. When he sensed nothing, he made his way to Richard's car and what had caught his attention. The car was parked on the street in front of his house and both tires that he could see had been slashed. Hacked, actually. Circling the car, he confirmed that the other two tires had received the same treatment. After taking a look around he headed back into the house, his previous concerns pushed to the back of his mind.

Taryn looked up in surprise when he came back in so quickly. "Did Richard come out yet?" he asked her.

"He just went into the kitchen." She stood, concern written on her face. He held a hand out to her and she took it, letting him lead her into the kitchen. Richard was leaning against the counter drinking from a coffee mug, both hands wrapped around the heat.

Caleb pulled a chair out for Taryn then sat down. "Richard, someone vandalized your car last night."

Surprise had Richard putting the mug down. "What?"

"Someone slashed your tires last night."

They stared at him for a moment then Richard pushed away from the counter and headed out of the kitchen, Taryn hot on his heels.

Richard led the way outside then stood on the walkway and stared at the car before looking at Caleb in confusion. Caleb took his hand and pulled him back inside the house. "You have AAA? It would be easiest to get a flatbed to take it to a tire shop."

"Yeah. You think I should call the police? My sister is on duty, I think."

"There's not much the police can do except take a report. I'm sorry, Rick, we don't often get vandalism in this neighborhood."

"Just one of those things, I guess. I'm going to take a shower, then I'll call."

"We'll call while you're in the shower, honey. And make breakfast." Taryn gave him a quick kiss and went to her purse. She pulled out the Automobile Association card and picked up the phone while Caleb started breakfast. They were just sitting down to eat, the tow truck promised within the hour, when the doorbell rang.

Caleb motioned the others to continue with their meals and went to answer the door. He raised his eyebrows in surprised inquiry to find Officer Laura Daniels and her partner Kevin on his porch, but the rest of him stilled as if bracing for impact. Clearly something was wrong.

"Caleb, long time no see."

"Laura, Kevin. Would you like to come in?"

"Richard's here?" she asked, stepping inside.

"In the kitchen."

He led the way back, going straight to the coffee to pour two mugs. Richard and Taryn stood up to greet the pair before they all took seats.

"Rick, have you been outside?"

"The tow truck is on its way."

Laura nodded then looked at him sympathetically. "I'm afraid there's more. Your house was vandalized last night. Since you weren't there, they called me and I thought you might be here, so we came over. When we saw the car, we realized it was more of a problem than we initially thought."

Richard's brow creased in confusion. "Vandalized how?"

Laura cleared her throat. "Spray paint on the house and a dead cat on the porch. It looks like it was road kill, not killed at your house."

"What the hell?" Richard shook his head in denial.

"What did the paint say?" Caleb asked, knowing there had to be more.

"It's not pretty."

Richard narrowed his eyes at his sister. "What did it say?"

"God will punish you."

Taryn's hand went to her mouth to stifle a cry of shock. Richard's fists clenched on the table. Caleb put his hand on Richard's shoulder and felt the muscles, tight and stiff.

"Officers are at the house, taking pictures. I called home and Brian's in town for the weekend. He and Dad are going to get some paint. They'll meet us at your house when we're done here."

Kevin cleared his throat. "Have you had any run-ins lately? With a patient? With anyone?"

"No."

Laura looked to Caleb and Taryn. "You guys experience anything weird? Have trouble with anyone?"

Caleb shook his head and Taryn answered negatively.

"No fights, nobody looking at you funny, nothing?"

All three indicated that there had been nothing. Laura focused her attention on Caleb. "The fact that they hit two different locations is not a good sign."

Caleb nodded, determined to maintain control despite the fury running through him. "They've either been following him or done a fair amount of research."

Richard was looking more and more upset. "You don't think it was random?"

"Either might have been random. Both is not." Laura nodded along with Caleb's assessment.

"I think you have a problem, Rick."

"Oh God." Richard stood up so fast his chair would have fallen over had Caleb not caught it. "The office!"

"I sent a car over. There was no sign of trouble," Laura reassured him.

Taryn and Caleb stood up, both putting a comforting hand on Richard. "We'll need to call and cancel the tow truck, I assume?" Caleb asked Laura.

"Yes, I'll send the guys at the house over here to take photos when they're done."

"Fine. We'll make some calls and head over to the house. Unless you'd rather wait here, Rick? We can get this done without you having to see it."

"No, I want to see."

They took Caleb's SUV to Richard's house. He asked Taryn to drive so that he could make phone calls from the back. Richard sat up front looking shell-shocked.

Keeping his voice low, Caleb called his employees. He sent one person to his house to set up video surveillance of the street with instructions to do the same at Richard's then go to the medical office and check the security set up there. He sent another to Taryn's apartment to check that nothing had happened and to maintain a personal watch. He had helped Richard upgrade his security system weeks ago and Taryn already had a top-of-the-line system that included both the shop and her apartment. When he was finished he took a minute to calm himself. He had been in many situations that had felt personal at the time, but nothing compared to this. This felt like an attack on his home, on his family.

"Richard, you go in and pack some things while we help get the painting done. As soon as it's finished we'll go to Taryn's so she can pack and we can check on the shop." Taryn pulled up to the curb at Richard's house. "We can pick up her car while we're there."

He opened the car door before realizing that they were both staring at him, Richard with irritation and Taryn with something more like anger.

"What?"

"What response are you expecting, Caleb?" Taryn asked, her tone biting. "Sir, yes sir?"

"Well, that would be nice, but a simple okay would work as well."

"Exactly what aspect of my personality has led you to believe that I am happy to follow orders willy-nilly?" Her glare was enough to warn him that he better be careful of his response.

"For fuck's sake, Taryn, this has nothing to do with the bedroom. I suggested the most obvious next move. I have the best security and the most space, so you should move in with me, at least until we figure out what the hell is going on here."

"Wow, what a charming offer, but I'm afraid I have a policy against roommates, let alone allowing other people's actions to make my decisions for me."

Caleb knew he was handling this badly but couldn't seem to stop himself. "Don't be a martyr, Tare. You need to be safe. I can provide that."

"My apartment and the shop are safe, they have excellent security, you said so yourself."

"Security, yes," he ground out through gritted teeth before making himself take a deep breath. "But considering anyone can walk in during business hours, that's hardly safe if someone is trying to hurt you."

"We have no reason to believe that anyone is trying to hurt me. And the only solution to that problem would be me not going to work at all." She sounded as frustrated as he did. "I'm not moving in with you because someone is vandalizing some of our property."

"How about moving in with me because you said you love me?"

"This isn't about you, Caleb, this is about Richard. He needs our help now, in case you hadn't noticed, not you being an overbearing ass." She didn't wait for a response, just slammed her way out of the car.

"That was," Richard paused, looking back at Caleb, "a very interesting way to ask the woman that you love to move in with you."

"Well I'm so sorry if my desire to keep you both safe is overbearing. And I asked you both, the two people I love, to move in with me." It was an effort to keep from yelling and Richard's relatively calm voice only pushed his anger higher.

"Well, it sounded more like you were offering your protective services, at least to me."

"Maybe because this morning you didn't fucking believe me when I told you I loved you."

"Fuck you, Caleb. Now is not the time for this." Richard got out and closed the door with a quiet snick.

"Son of a bitch." The words were barely whispered as Caleb tried to figure out what the hell had happened. He was a trained soldier for fuck's sake. He knew how to handle himself under pressure. He knew how to lead his team through a mission successfully and safely. What he had suggested was the most obvious next step. Period.

His phone rang and he answered it while finally getting out of the car. He looked around and saw that Richard was talking to a small army of people who were probably his family. Caleb had not yet met any of Richard's family or Taryn's friends other than at the shop, something he had been hoping to discuss with both of them today. Maybe he had been vastly overrating their commitment to him and this relationship. The very idea pissed him off further. He was *not* used to second guessing himself, damn it. Taryn, he noticed, was standing next to the group, but to the side, staring at the ugly words painted on the house.

Kevin approached him when he hung up the phone, as his partner was in the middle of explaining something to the group. "They're a good family, very close. This is going to piss them off."

"I wouldn't know, I haven't met them."

"Oh, sorry. I guess I thought you guys were pretty tight, but I know it hasn't been long."

"Yeah. Well. Have they found anything helpful?" He gestured toward the black and white that was now leaving, hopefully having collected some evidence.

"Not really."

"Great."

"This is probably nothing. Just some jackass kids."

"Yeah, jackass kids love to invoke God in their Friday night spray painting parties," Caleb answered, his voice tight.

"We had a car drive by the coffee shop but everything looked normal."

"I sent someone out there."

Kevin nodded and headed back over to his partner. Caleb followed along, getting there in time to hear the man he assumed was Richard's father. "Why don't you stay with us for a couple of days while your sister looks into this? Taryn, you could stay as well, you know we'd love to have you."

"I'll stay where I was last night, it's plenty safe, Dad." He looked around, gesturing as he spotted Caleb's arrival. "This is Caleb. It happens he's in the security business, so his house is very secure. Mom, Dad, everyone, this is Caleb. Caleb, this is my mother Sylvia, my father Don, my brother Brian, his girlfriend Callie, my cousin Clara and her husband Steve."

Caleb shook the hands closest to him and attempted a smile. "It's nice to meet you all."

"It's so nice of you to *ask*, Don." Taryn gave a significant look to Caleb. "But this is very minor, there's no reason to believe that anyone is in danger and Caleb has already vetted my security system, so there's no reason to put you out."

"Don't be silly," Sylvia chided, coming to put her arm around Taryn. "You know we love to have you at the house. We miss having you kids around. We can have a good dinner at the restaurant then go home and pop popcorn and watch movies like we used to do when you came home from college."

Caleb had never seen Taryn so…reserved. He wondered if that was due to her being pissed off at him, or if she didn't particularly care for Richard's family. She had never said anything bad about them but that didn't mean she liked them.

Taryn announced she was going inside for a drink and asked if anyone else wanted something. Caleb's phone rang again and he moved off to answer it.

Chapter Nine
✆

Taryn needed to calm down. Caleb had likely not meant for his words to be taken as an order. Probably, if she had actually voiced another suggestion he would have listened. She would never know, because she hadn't really had another suggestion. What she had was a knee-jerk reaction to people telling her what to do. Well, outside of the bedroom anyway. This was why she owned her own business, rather than working for someone else.

But she was uncomfortable, as she always was around Richard's family, which made it harder to let her mad go. They were good people. They'd worked hard to help her feel welcome since the day they met her and had tried to make her feel like family since the day they realized she and Richard were more than friends. She just…wasn't comfortable with families. Didn't really know what to do with them.

At first she had tried to keep her distance because what was the point of getting to know people who lived in another state? When she moved here she was focused on getting her shop open and settled, not making friends. At least, that's what she told Richard the first dozen times he asked her to join him at family functions. She joined him occasionally and liked them well enough, she just didn't feel like one of them. Didn't want to feel like one of them.

She had her friends and her employees and her customers. She had Richard. She didn't need his family, too. Now she had Caleb. Crap. How had they gone from saying "I love you" last night to this? She knew he was probably pissed at how she had overreacted in the car but she was damned if she was going to move in with the guy because he decided it would keep her safe. Although, to be perfectly fair, she wouldn't have moved in with him for any other reason, either. What was the point? They saw enough of each other now, they had plenty of sex. And if he liked someone in his bed every damn night, then wasn't it lucky that he had Richard, too? Aargh! She was making herself crazy.

Richard's dad was getting the painting organized and he handed her a brush. "You okay, sweetie?"

"I'm good, Don, thanks. It was nice of you all to come out here like this."

"Of course, that's what family is for." He paused, ducked his head. "You know, uh... You know that if you all want to stay at the house, Sylvia and I, we won't be real particular on who, you know, stays in what room." He blushed but managed to look her in the eye.

Taryn felt her heart go soft. Richard was lucky to have such caring parents who put their son's happiness in such high regard. "You're a good guy, Don. Thank you. But I don't see any reason that's necessary. We'll be just fine. I know Sylvia wishes otherwise, but I'm afraid we're just not kids anymore." She gave him a wry smile and he laughed.

"Well, she'd probably forgive you for that if at least one of you would get around to having some kids of your own so she can start the spoiling all over again."

Taryn opened her eyes wide and gave him her best over-the-top horrified look, getting another laugh out of him. She took the paintbrush and went to the wall. It had been determined that the paint they had was close enough in color to the house that they could just paint the one side, for now. The whole house could use a new paint job, but Richard didn't want to decide on a new color scheme now. With the number of people involved it would take no time at all to do just the one side.

She looked over and found Caleb and Richard coming to paint on either side of her. She waited to see if it would make her feel claustrophobic but she felt fine. Losing herself in the easy rhythms, she thought back to her dinner with Petra last night.

Petra had quizzed her on her relationship with Caleb and Richard. She had always pushed for a stronger relationship between Taryn and Richard, despite fixing him up with her gay friends when Taryn was dating other men. She had been a little hesitant at first, unsure about Caleb's addition but Taryn had told her how happy he made both her and Richard. By the time they finished with drinks and moved on to dinner Petra was happy for them and pushing for sexy details, with Emma egging her on. Taryn managed to get away with only a few teasing comments. Why had she been so happy and in love last night and then so pissed off this morning?

The painting was finished quickly and Richard handed their brushes to Caleb and pulled Taryn to the SUV. She was suddenly very tired and rested her forehead against his shoulder as he leaned against the truck and brushed the hair back from her face.

"You got up awfully early this morning, sweetie, considering we were up so late."

Taryn sighed. "You think I'm doing it again, but I'm not. Hell, I told him I loved him last night. And I meant it. I can't help it if I like my alone time."

"You do have a tendency to pull away from a guy just as things start to get serious," he reminded her. "Sweetie, you know I don't think there's anything wrong with liking your own space now and then. But you're not being fair if you're implying we've done anything to restrict that." He frowned. "Look, I don't know what's going to happen here but I feel like I want to milk it for everything I can. This is something special and I want to enjoy it for as long as possible. Don't you want that?"

"I am enjoying it. I love you. I love him. It's all good. So what's the problem?"

"The problem," Caleb growled from behind her, "is that you're holding back. You both are."

Taryn felt Richard stiffen in surprise and realized they had both missed his approach. She kept her head where it was, her eyes closed. "Yes, well. What, exactly, is wrong with that? It's only natural. It's been an amazing few weeks, but it has been only weeks."

"You said you loved me. And that you trusted me. I thought that meant something." She felt him step closer so that they were in a tight group, like that very first night.

"It does. It means I love you. And that I trust you. It doesn't mean I give my life to you. It doesn't mean you can just order me around because I love you."

"It wasn't an order."

"It sounded like one."

"Fine, then I apologize for that. But it has nothing to do with the fact that you're both holding back." She opened her eyes, unhappy to hear the weary frustration in his voice. He ran a hand through his hair and glanced over at the crowd. "Can we go inside to talk about this?"

Taryn looked up at Richard. "Would you rather stay here or go somewhere else?"

"I don't want to smell paint right now. Let's go back to Caleb's house."

Taryn climbed into the driver's seat while Richard thanked everyone. Caleb got into the front passenger seat and looked at her. "I am sorry."

"Fine. I appreciate that." He continued to watch and she sighed and turned to face him. "I'm sorry I overreacted. It's a pet peeve of mine."

"How come I haven't heard about it until now?"

Taryn looked at him closely to see if he was being a smart ass but she couldn't tell. "Because it hasn't come up. Because you haven't pushed that button."

He just nodded his head and looked forward as Richard climbed into the backseat. She started the car and pulled out as the last of Richard's family drove away.

Caleb spoke up as they neared the main street. "Does anyone feel like cooking or should we get some lunch to take ho...back to the house?"

"I definitely do not feel like cooking." Taryn slowed and pulled over to the curb.

"Me neither. Why don't I run into the deli real quick?" Richard suggested, pointing to the small shop across the street from where she had stopped.

Caleb and Taryn agreed then watched him as he crossed the street. Caleb waited until he had entered the deli before speaking.

"You don't like Richard's family?"

Taryn frowned. "They're nice people. Very loving and supportive of Richard. Of each other."

"So why don't you like them?"

"I like them just fine. They're Richard's family, not my friends."

She watched him out of the corner of her eye, refusing to give him her full attention.

"Why does it make you uncomfortable?"

"I don't know, why don't you tell me?" She was mad again. Damn it, what was his problem today?

"So there's nothing I should be concerned about? On his behalf?"

"What do you mean?" She looked at him now, confused.

He shrugged his shoulders, his expression even. "I mean, I love him. If they treat him badly or put unusual stress on him for some reason, I want to know about it."

She turned back, facing forward. "No," she said softly. "They're very good to him. Like I said, they're a good family. He's lucky to have them."

111

"Okay. Thanks."

She just nodded, having no idea why she was choked up.

Richard's car was gone from the street when they got back to Caleb's house. They went inside and sat down to eat without saying much. Taryn was barely able to force down half her sandwich. She wrapped the rest up and put it in the fridge. She stared inside, seeing her favorite drinks, the cheese she preferred that Caleb hated. In her mind, she saw the load of her clothes in the washer that she had started that morning, reminding herself she needed to transfer it to the dryer. She saw the extra bottle of shampoo and conditioner she'd bought rather than continue to bring them from her house or Richard's where an identical set remained.

She felt drained, defeated somehow. Last night had been so wonderful. Nothing had changed really and yet she felt so afraid. She was thirty-one years old and she was afraid of...what? Love? How pathetic was she?

Warm hands drew her back from the open refrigerator. She kept her head down as she realized that tears were threatening to fall. Richard's hand lifted her chin, brushing her hair back so he could see her face. Caleb's hands rubbed up and down her arms, warming her chilled skin.

"I love you." Richard's quiet statement broke her control. At her first sob, Caleb scooped her up and walked her into the living room. He and Richard sat on the couch together, draping her across their laps. They held her tight while she cried.

"Oh sweetie. You're killing me here." Richard's voice was full of soft concern while Caleb's hands held her to him, her head on his chest.

"I don't..." she hiccuped. "I don't cry," she managed before full racking sobs overtook her. Richard scooted even closer, practically sitting on Caleb's lap with her.

"Tell us what's wrong." Caleb's voice was soothing while his grip was almost painful.

"I don't know."

"Yes you do."

"I'm scared."

"Of the vandal?" Richard sounded surprised.

Taryn didn't answer.

"Taryn."

"Caleb."

"Tell us."

"You're telling me what to do again." She tried not to sound petulant.

"This is different. Don't pretend otherwise."

"I'm scared."

"I know," Caleb said patiently.

"Taryn."

"Richard."

"You must know we won't let anyone hurt you."

"What if you hurt me?"

"You can't mean that." He sounded shocked and hurt.

"You told me you love me. Caleb told me he loved me."

"I've told you I loved you before. Lots of times."

"This is different," she insisted.

"Yes, it is. But it's supposed to be good different, not scary different."

"You got scared," Caleb pointed out to Richard. This got Taryn's attention and she looked up at Richard.

"Yes, well, that's different too."

Taryn wrinkled her brow. "Why did you get scared? This is everything you've wanted."

"Isn't it everything you've wanted?"

"I guess...I guess it's everything I said I wanted. Maybe even what I thought I wanted."

Richard pulled back. "You're telling me now that you don't want it, even though it's pretty fucking perfect, and you don't expect me to get scared? Of course I'm scared, I'm fucking terrified you guys have made me fall in love with you and you're going to take it away."

"That's what I'm saying! Shit happens, you can't expect perfect to last. It doesn't last, it never does!"

"It's one thing for it not to last, for whatever reason," Richard yelled, getting to his feet, nearly dislodging Taryn. "It's totally different when perfect moves down the road, sets up housekeeping and leaves you behind."

"What the hell does that mean?" Taryn struggled out of Caleb's arms and they both stood up to face Richard.

"It means how do you think I'm going to be able to stand it if you guys get married and move into the perfect house, in the perfect neighborhood and start the perfect family?"

"There's no such thing as perfect! That's why this is so scary, because it can't last. Something will fuck it up. But I figured it would be something else, some outside thing screwing with us, not you insulting me! How could you think that I would ditch you for him? I've loved you for years. You're my best friend, the only person who has loved me for a long time and you think I'm just going to throw that away!"

"Yes, you love me like a friend, you always have. But look at him!" Richard gestured to Caleb who was standing very still. "No such thing as perfect, my ass! We've never met anyone who's so perfect for us—of course you're going to want to have it all with him. I said we would remain friends but how hard do you think that's going to be for me, to sit back and watch you create a family with him?"

"For fuck's sake, Richard, I don't want a family! If I wanted a family I would have joined yours, years ago. And if I did want one with him, why wouldn't you be there with us? You keep saying that like I'm going to choose him over you. Where would you get an idea like that? You're insulting both of us. Besides, where would you get the idea that he would choose me over you?"

They were both fairly close to screaming now. Taryn's tears were falling unchecked but now they were tears of anger. "This..." she pointed at Richard. "This is why I don't want a family. If the person I love and trust most in the world doesn't trust me, why would I choose to give myself to anyone else?"

Caleb stepped forward. "Enough." He pulled them both in close and Taryn thought about struggling but her anger drained from her suddenly and it was all she could do to remain standing. "Enough," Caleb whispered again, tightening his grip on them both. Taryn's arms went around him and Richard's went around both of them. They stood that way until their breathing had evened out.

Finally Caleb took them each by the hand and began pulling them toward the bedroom.

"Caleb." Taryn knew she sounded unsure.

"Taryn."

She gestured toward the bedroom with her free hand, then let it drop.

"Shh, it's going to be fine. We're all tired, we need a nap."

"You're telling us what to do again." She wasn't angry and knew she didn't sound it so she wasn't surprised when he just smiled back at her.

"I know. I think I know the difference now, but you be sure and point out to me if I get it wrong, okay?"

She rolled her eyes at his back. When they got to the bed he left them standing at the foot while he closed all the drapes and turned on the ceiling fan. He pulled the covers back on the bed then undressed Richard. Kissing him lightly on the lips, Caleb ushered him under the covers then turned to her. He undressed her with a minimum of fuss, as he had done Richard, then gave her a light kiss too before urging her into bed. Richard opened his arms to her and she snuggled in, laying her head on his chest. The bed sagged behind her as

Caleb joined them, spooning her back, draping his leg over both hers and Richard's, his arm coming over her to rest on Richard's chest.

"Sleep," was his last command, or at least the last she was awake for.

Chapter Ten

ജ

Richard woke from their nap feeling better. How could he not feel good with Taryn draped over him and Caleb snuggled in close? They were probably both still pissed at him but here they were, wrapping him up in their heat. Taryn shifted a bit and he paid close attention to what her knee was doing until she stilled again. It wouldn't be the first time she kneed him in her sleep.

Running a hand down her back, he let it rest at her waist. He needed to talk to her about what she had been yelling about. It wasn't rare for them to squabble, but it was rare for them to fight like they had that afternoon. He'd been stunned to hear her talk as if she didn't expect her relationship with Caleb to last. He had honestly thought she was imagining getting married, though they hadn't discussed it. Hell, this was what she had always wanted, what *they* had always wanted. Now she was saying she didn't want a family? Color him confused.

Richard rolled his head to look up at Caleb who was sharing the same pillow. Caleb's eyes were open and steady on him. Richard gulped at his lover's expression. He looked...disappointed. And sad. Feeling ashamed but not exactly sure why, Richard looked away and closed his eyes. His arms tightened accidentally on Taryn and she stirred. Lifting her head, she saw that they were both awake and moved off Richard to sit cross-legged. Seeing Caleb's expression, she flushed and looked down at her knees.

"Richard, you want to tell me where you got the idea that we were going to dump you and get married?"

"Uh. Well. Logic, I guess."

117

"Not good enough."

"What do you want me to say? Of course you didn't say or do anything, but that doesn't mean it's not what's going to happen." Knowing he sounded belligerent only made him more defensive.

"Taryn's right, I find that very insulting."

Richard sat up, leaning against the headboard, pulling his knees in close.

"Taryn."

Taryn's heavy sigh spoke volumes.

"Caleb."

"I love you."

Taryn's shoulders slumped and her sullen expression vanished as tears threatened to fall, unnerving Richard.

"Damn it." She shook her head.

"I'm sorry, it may not be easy for you to hear, baby, but I do. So does Richard, and whether you like it or not, so does his entire family. I'm willing to bet you can add Emma and Petra to the list too, and those are just the people I can think of off the top of my head. I have no doubt there are more."

"Stop it."

"No."

"Of course my family loves you. Why would you think they didn't?" Richard asked, confused. "And what's this about not wanting a family? Isn't that what you've always wanted?"

"I thought I did, I was wrong. Your family is super nice and polite to me because they love you, that's all."

"Your parents dying had nothing to do with how much they loved you," Caleb said quietly.

"Oh please, what? Are you a fucking psychologist now?"

"It doesn't take a psychologist to figure it out when you were shouting it to us an hour ago."

"I didn't say anything about my parents. And their dying had nothing to do with me. It had to do with the piece of shit who left his car on the tracks and killed them."

Richard felt like he was playing catch-up. "Then you went to live with your grandmother, which wasn't the greatest."

"Not everyone get's greatest, but it wasn't bad. I'm not complaining about 'wasn't bad'."

"She was a drunk."

"Lots of people are."

"And so was your aunt."

"Again, lots of people are. Look, I don't know what you guys are trying to imply. I wasn't beaten or starved."

"You weren't loved," Richard said with understanding.

"My parents loved me."

"Until they died." Caleb said it straight out and Richard watched Taryn's face tighten even further.

"Whatever." She unfolded her legs and made to get up but Caleb reached out and grabbed one ankle and Richard grabbed the other.

"We love you."

"It's not that simple."

"Why not?"

"I don't know, Richard, why not? Why don't you tell me? An hour ago you were telling me my love for you wasn't good enough."

Richard blushed. "That's not what I said."

"It sounded a whole lot like that. You didn't believe that my love for you was as strong as my love for Caleb, which is only weeks old. What does that say about me and my ability to love and be loved?"

"All right, let's not start screaming again." Caleb interrupted, earning glares from both of them. "This is obviously all my fault."

Taryn narrowed her eyes at him and Richard wondered what was coming next.

"Neither of you trusts me. That's a little…hard for me to take. I thought we'd gotten way beyond that. I forgot that trusting me with your bodies, even your hearts, is not the same as trusting me with your futures. I'm sorry I pushed. I shouldn't have said that last night I guess. It wasn't meant to be a burden."

Caleb got up off the bed and left the room. Richard looked at Taryn.

"Everything seemed so easy," he said.

"Until it wasn't," she agreed.

"Yeah. I'm going to take a shower."

Letting the water wash over him didn't seem to help. Logically, he knew that neither Caleb nor Taryn had said or done anything to give him the impression that they wanted to be a couple without him. He knew it was his own assumptions and insecurities, but that didn't make them any harder to put away. Replacing Caleb's shampoo on the little ledge next to Taryn's, it occurred to him that he hadn't brought over many personal items to this house. Taryn had, and she frequently left extras at his house as well.

And yet she was the one who refused to spend more than a couple of nights away from home. She was the one who didn't invite them to her apartment, preferring to come to their houses. Her excuse that they had a lot more room than her apartment suddenly struck him as just that, an excuse. Why had he never noticed that about her? He was supposed to be her closest friend yet he hadn't even realized she was keeping herself apart.

Shit, maybe they did need therapy. Couples therapy. His laugh did not exactly sound amused as he turned off the water. Stepping into the room while toweling off, he met Caleb coming in.

"I'm going to take my run now. You want to come?"

They had jogged together a couple of times and Richard had enjoyed it. Caleb clearly held his pace back but they'd had some good conversations.

"Sure."

They started out at the pace they had found comfortable the last time they'd run together. Richard found the combination of exertion and peaceful surroundings compelling. He found himself thinking about how he hadn't invited Caleb to his family's restaurant, nor introduced Caleb to his parents. They had only gone on a few actual dates, preferring to spend their time together at Caleb or Richard's house. Knowing, vaguely, that he was holding part of himself back had seemed smart. Now it seemed unfair. Like he was cheating. Cheating the very people he was claiming to love.

It wasn't until they neared the house that Richard realized he had increased his pace, as if running away from the hard truths. He was gasping for breath and tried to be impressed, rather than irritated, that Caleb was barely breathing heavily. Whatever, at least he got to enjoy that body. He'd just have to think of other ways to make the man pant. They walked the last half block, cooling down, Caleb shooting glances at him now and then. When they reached the yard Richard braced his hands on his knees until he was breathing normally. Finally he stood up and looked Caleb in the eye. It wasn't easy, but he said it. "I'm sorry."

Caleb blinked, his face clearing of all expression. "For what?"

"For not trusting you. For telling you I loved you but not being willing to give you all of myself in return."

Caleb's eyes closed for a minute then opened again. Their heat seared him straight to the soul. "And now?"

"I feel like I'm jumping off a cliff. It's scary as hell, no safety net."

"It's also a rush."

"Yeah. Yeah, it is that." Reaching out, he grabbed Caleb's waist and drew him in. Eyes locked, they met each other halfway. Richard moaned at the feel of Caleb's warm lips and wet tongue. The smell of sweaty man made him even hotter.

"Do I need to turn on the sprinklers?" Taryn's voice reached them from the front door and they pulled away, laughing.

Caleb caught his arm before he could head up to the house. "Thank you."

"For apologizing?"

"For trying."

Richard nodded. "I need to apologize to Taryn too. Not just for my thing, but for not even realizing she was having a problem."

"I think she's pretty good at hiding it, even from herself."

"Then it's a good thing she has two of us to keep an eye on her."

Caleb laughed and shoved him toward the door. "I don't think I'd mention that to her, if I were you."

"Duh."

When they reached the door Taryn was standing behind, she said, "Ugh, you boys need another shower." She pushed the door shut behind them, revealing her naked self. "I think I'll join you. Save water, you know."

"Social responsibility is so sexy," Caleb said, snatching her up and throwing her over his shoulder as she shrieked at him.

After they showered and managed to get dressed again, Richard ushered them into the living room. He kneeled in front of Taryn, sitting on the couch. "Sweetie, I'm so sorry that I was holding back on this new relationship. I can't promise that I'll have it all figured out now, but I promise I will try to open my whole heart to it. I was afraid of loving you guys too much, afraid of how it was going to hurt if it didn't work out.

But I'm done with that. I love you. I love him." Trying not to be upset at the panicked look on Taryn's face, Richard looked to Caleb.

Caleb quirked an eyebrow. "Gee, all I got was an, 'I'm sorry, Caleb'." They all laughed and Richard figured now was not the time to tackle Taryn's issues. At least not verbally. He had another plan entirely for that. Standing, he yanked her to her feet as well.

"Let's go to dinner, I'm starved and we haven't been to Mama's in ages." Turning to Caleb, he said, "Will you come meet my family properly?"

Caleb nodded. "I'd love to." They didn't give the sputtering Taryn much notice as they dragged her outside.

"Maybe I don't feel like Italian."

"You know Pop will make you whatever you want." He shoved her into the SUV and closed the door on whatever protest she was forming. By the time he climbed in, intentionally taking the long way around to the other side, she was silent.

When Caleb pulled into the parking lot he glanced back at Richard. Sitting forward on his seat, Richard leaned against hers until he could see her face.

"You've never had a problem coming here before."

"I know."

"If you really don't want to go inside, that's fine, we can go somewhere else. But I think we need to talk about what the problem is."

She gave him her most irritated look and he had to bite his tongue not to laugh. She was just too damn cute. "I'm hungry," she said, opening her door. By the time Richard got out and made it around to their side of the truck, Caleb had Taryn frozen with a kiss. Richard moved up, covering her back, showing her with what he had that he was there for her, that they were both there for her. He put his arms around her stomach, holding her close. Caleb's hands were cupping her face and Richard moved in to nuzzle the other man's hands on her cheek. Caleb moved one hand to thread his fingers through Richard's hair and Richard turned in to join the kiss. It was an awkward angle and they broke apart, laughing.

"Fine, whatever. Let's eat." Taryn pushed through them and headed for the door.

Chapter Eleven

ഔ

Caleb had to admit that he was a bit nervous coming to eat at Mama's. Luckily he could concentrate on Taryn's issues and pretend he was totally fine. Mentally kicking his ass for feeling hurt that Richard hadn't invited him here before when he hadn't exactly gone out of his way to introduce them to his family either, he straightened his shoulders and prepared to do the family thing. The truth was he didn't actually have much experience in this regard. He had never taken a date "home" and had never allowed anyone he was seeing to take him home, either.

Watching Richard hug his cousin Clara who stood at the hostess stand, Caleb leaned into Taryn. "Maybe Chinese would have been good, now that I think this through."

Glad to see that she was straining to keep from laughing at him, he gave her a comically nervous look.

"I tried to warn you, meeting the parents is scary stuff." She slung her arm as far up to his shoulders as she could reach and gave an exaggerated sigh. "It's okay, baby, I'm here for you."

Caleb couldn't resist bending down to kiss her. Which was, of course, the perfect time for Richard's parents to show up.

"Welcome, welcome." Sylvia Daniels gave him a motherly hug before turning him over to her husband for similar treatment. So at least they were welcoming, not suspicious or judgmental. He could deal with this. Right? He would just stick close to Taryn, make sure she was doing okay.

As they all took their seats at a large table in a semi-private room, it occurred to Caleb that the only reason he hadn't been nervous about this, like Taryn, was because he was an idiot. He seriously had not given the reality of being on the receiving end of this much curiosity and protective instinct the attention it deserved. Reminding himself to do some major apologizing to her at the earliest possible chance, he tried to draw on his training to at least ensure that his fear was not actually showing.

Despite his brief pessimism—well, okay, fear—the Danielses put a great deal of effort into making him feel comfortable at their table. They told stories about Richard as a kid and even about Richard and Taryn's visits home during college. It was quickly clear to him that the whole family made a project out of convincing Taryn that she was one of them. Now that he thought about it, he was somewhat surprised they didn't see him as a threat to that goal. Laughing at a story Richard was telling about Laura's first day on the police force, he finally relaxed.

When dessert was brought to the table, Caleb stared at it, trying to convince himself his body could somehow hold another couple of bites. Richard brought up the vandalism, asking his sister if there had been any updates.

"Nothing yet, it's too early for any lab results, and I'm not really optimistic about those anyway." Frowning, she shook her head. "I don't know, brother, it seems personal, like you should know what it's about and who it might be."

Richard glanced at Caleb, his frown matching his sister's.

Richard's father spoke up. "Do you think it might be..." He paused, gesturing to the three of them. He looked embarrassed but was obviously not willing to ignore the elephant at the table if it meant danger to his son. "I don't know, some idiot concerned about your love life?"

"I don't know, Dad. I can't imagine."

"What are you going to do?" Sylvia asked.

Caleb cleared his throat. "I've set up some surveillance in case they come back. In the meantime we'll all just be very aware of our surroundings and anybody who strikes us as odd. I have a lot of resources in that area so we can check out anyone we're concerned about, no matter how unlikely. You should all do the same, actually. It can't hurt for everyone here to be extra aware. You can send any information about suspicious people to me and I'll have my people check them out." He nodded at Laura. "Unlike the police, I don't have to worry about stepping on anyone's toes."

Everyone nodded their agreement to that as they finished their desserts.

As they made ready to leave, every single one of the Daniels clan made a point of saying goodbye and showing their acceptance of both Caleb and Taryn. He was damn near choked up by the time they exited the restaurant and made it to the car.

The ride home was quiet, each caught up in their own thoughts.

"I need to do a little work on the computer before I turn in," Richard said, and headed to the office.

"I'm tired, I'm going to bed." Taryn yawned and headed to the master bedroom.

Caleb took the leftovers into the kitchen and set up the coffee pot to turn on in the morning, since they all had early starts for the next day. He double-checked the house to make sure everything was locked up, even though he knew it already was. He stopped at the door to the office. Richard had made himself at home at the desk, he was pleased to see.

He walked in and Richard looked up.

"Caleb."

"Ricky, you look tired," Caleb said.

Richard's smile was wry. "I am, believe me, I'll be done in a minute."

"Good." He leaned down and kissed Richard's cheek then left him to it.

When he got to the bedroom he could see that despite their nap, Taryn was sleepy. She usually propped up against the headboard to read but now she was already lying down, her eyes half closed as she read her paperback.

"Richard said he wouldn't be long," he told her as he stripped down to his boxers. Putting her book away, she waited until he had climbed in and was resting against the headboard so that she could snuggle against him.

"You were right," he told her. "That was scary." She sighed, melting into him, resting her head against his chest so that he could feel her warm breath against his skin.

"But being brave is about doing it even when it's scary." He felt the smile that curved her lips, even though he couldn't see it, as she echoed his earlier words.

"Brat. Well then, we were brave tonight. Or you were, since I wasn't smart enough to be scared until it was too late."

She burrowed in closer. "But you were scared in an immediate, 'they could really hate me and make my life miserable' way. I've got this whole rest of my life thing going on. I guess I need to figure that out."

"You think?"

Without looking, she reached up and bopped him on the head.

"Hey, violence is not the answer."

"Whatever."

Richard came back in, rubbing his eyes in fatigue. He watched them as he shucked his jeans. "Thanks for tonight. I hope it wasn't excruciating."

"You know it wasn't. Your family is too awesome to leave anyone uncomfortable in their presence for long," Taryn chided him.

"Well, you've proved a unique challenge to them for a long time."

"I wasn't uncomfortable with them. I just didn't want to be absorbed by them."

"And now?"

Groaning, she rose from her position on Caleb's chest so that she could see them both. "And now I see that they are a very important part of who you are, and since you are a very important part of who I am, I need to make peace with the fact that they are stuck with me and I am stuck with them."

Richard grimaced. "Is it that bad?"

"No, honey, you know it's not. I was just being neurotic. You have an awesome family and I'm lucky that you come as a package deal. I'm sorry I haven't realized that before now, I didn't mean to make things difficult for you."

"You didn't." He kissed her as he joined them on the bed. "I guess now, looking back on it, it's just one of the things that kept us as friends and lovers, but not partners. One out of many. We weren't ready. Obviously we needed an overbearing asshole to really pull the whole thing together."

Caleb growled and launched himself at Richard. Laughing, Richard dodged at the last second, ending up on his side instead of his back. Caleb still would have had the advantage had Taryn not joined Richard in pushing him to his back. He debated toppling them both versus letting them have their way but lost his train of thought as two hands, one small, one large, reached inside his boxers at the same time, clearly intent on the same goal.

Remaining still, he waited to see what they would do. Richard shoved his shoulder, encouraging him to lie back all the way.

"You're ours," Taryn said, her free hand pulling his shorts down.

"And we want to play," Richard added, giving him a squeeze.

He collapsed back and lifted his hips, deciding to let them have their way. At least for now.

Releasing Caleb's dick to Taryn's mercy, Richard moved up to kiss him, hard and demanding. Caleb's heart raced as the other man fisted his fingers through his hair while he attacked his mouth, in direct opposition to the sweet, tender torture Taryn was performing down below. Her hands were like silk on his rock-hard shaft as she peppered tiny kisses up his thighs, coming ever closer to his balls.

He tried to shout when hard fingers tweaked and pulled his nipples at the exact moment wet heat enveloped his aching balls, but the fierce kiss left little room for breathing let alone speaking. When Taryn's sweet mouth moved up his shaft to the head, he couldn't hold back. Using his hands to tear Richard's mouth from his, he looked the other man in the eye. "I want to taste you." Richard's breath hitched and he scrambled up, knees to either side of Caleb's head.

Caleb braced one hand on Richard's hip and used the other to feed himself warm cock. He had to be careful not to bite down when Taryn's tongue teased his slit. Using his own tongue, he thoroughly wetted the cock he held captive, his hand at the base squeezing tightly. Richard's groan seemed to egg Taryn on and she began to fuck him with her mouth. He hummed his own appreciation and Richard couldn't keep from pumping himself into Caleb. Caleb let him, his hand on the man's hip keeping his pace in check as his own hips began to thrust.

Taryn used one hand to tease the skin behind his balls. Caleb groaned, the vibration proving too much for Richard who came with a shout. Caleb swallowed him down until he was empty then gently pushed him away and let his own orgasm wash through him with a shout. He heard Taryn's cry of release and rolled his head to watch her, eyes closed in pleasure as her hand dropped away from between her legs.

He very nearly didn't have the energy to sit up, but reminded himself that he was a tough guy, in excellent shape. He shoved Richard over and kissed him, loving the taste of Richard, double. Then he pushed the man up toward the pillows and turned toward his woman. She was almost asleep already, cracking her eyes open when he leaned over her. Pulling her fingers into his mouth, he cleaned her juices off before giving her a kiss. "Good girl." He pushed her toward Richard then collapsed beside her, one arm over her head, playing with Richard's hair, the other over her waist, resting on Richard's hip.

* * * * *

The next morning, Taryn was already out of bed when Caleb woke up. He left Richard to sleep a little bit longer and took a shower. When the door opened, he accepted a sleepy kiss and helped her shampoo her hair, but refrained from any activity that might make her late.

While Richard took his turn in the shower and Taryn worked in the other bathroom to dry her hair, Caleb made breakfast. It was nice to open the refrigerator and find so many choices. He didn't mind cooking but grocery shopping was another story. Taryn, however, seemed to prefer to do the shopping, load the fridge and stand back while others produced meals from the food she'd selected.

The system was working well for all of them, he decided as he sautéed some onions and mushrooms for omelets. When the others joined him at the table, he squelched the brief impulse to bring up topics heavier than breakfast and morning schedules. It was time for him to do what he had accused them of not doing, treat this relationship as if it were permanent. Until he could honestly say he was doing that, he had no room to call them on their own hesitant behaviors.

They finished breakfast and headed out the door. Caleb dropped Richard and Taryn off in front of the coffee shop then drove to work. He checked with all his people as well as the surveillance tapes and found nothing helpful. He was carefully observant of his people, alert to any looks of distaste or even irritation, but saw nothing. He put in some hours on one project then drove out to an office building on the edge of town for another. By the time he was finished it was late afternoon and he had skipped lunch. He squared his shoulders and entered *Roisin Dubh*, reminding himself that he was a badass, and while his brother's approval would be nice, it certainly wasn't necessary.

A quick look around found Sean behind the bar and no sign of Lisa. By the time he got to the bar his brother had a glass of soda waiting for him.

"Want some lunch? I have some of mom's meatloaf."

"That would be perfect, thanks." Taking the soda, he moved to a table and sat down. Sean joined him quickly with two plates of meatloaf. They ate in silence, rolling their eyes at the antics of some college students nearby playing with the juke box.

Finally pushing the plate away, Caleb eyed his brother. They hadn't talked sex in a very long time, not since his older brother had shoved a handful of condoms at him when he was thirteen and told him to always be smart.

"I'm thinking of moving into the house. The renters' lease is up next month."

"You said you had some guys at work who might want to rent it."

"They'll find another place."

Sean got up and came back with a glass of water.

"Like you've said all along, it's too much house for one person."

"Probably even too much house for two people, especially if they're sharing a bedroom."

Sean's lips quirked. "Yeah? How 'bout three people?"

"Probably they would need more space, whether they're sharing a room or not," Caleb answered carefully.

Nodding his head, Sean only said, "Probably." Then he lost his cool and gave his brother a pained look. "So, guys, huh?"

Caleb just shrugged. "In general, very rarely. Specifically, and with her, yeah. It works. It's right." Taking a long drink, he watched for a reaction but got only a small nod. "You knew?"

It was Sean's turn to shrug. "You weren't exactly hiding it."

"No. But I'd understand if you were...uncomfortable."

"Look, I won't lie and say I get it. Mostly I'd rather just not think about it in too much detail. But I hardly see what other people get up to in the bedroom as having anything to do with me."

Caleb nodded. "And if it goes beyond the bedroom?" He laughed at Sean's confused expression. "These people are important to me. Like family, I hope."

"Oh. Right. Well, I don't see why that would be a problem. I mean, if you like them that much, chances are we will, too." He cleared his throat. "Why don't you, you know, bring them to the pub for drinks and dinner. We can work our way up to dinner at the house."

"Actually, we met here."

Sean looked at him, goggle-eyed. Caleb barely kept from laughing. "Well, outside. They were a little bit too full of your spirits and needed a hand."

"Well, okay then. Shows they have good taste."

Caleb stood and picked up his plate and glass, leading the way back to the kitchen. He put the dishes in the sink and turned to his brother, pulling him in for a hug. "I'll call you, figure out a date. I have to warn you though, Richard's got a little bit of a crush on Lisa."

"Oh, well, see. Like I said, good taste."

"That's what I told him." He slapped his brother on the back and headed outside. Putting on his sunglasses, he took a careful look around. Nothing unusual caught his eye, nobody appeared to be focusing their attention on him. He drove to

Richard's medical office on full alert. Parking on the street, he watched the busy afternoon traffic, both cars and pedestrians.

About to get out and go into the coffee shop, he paused when his phone rang. When he saw that it was Taryn he couldn't hold back his grin.

"Taryn."

"Caleb, hey. I was just, well, ummm..." She sighed and he could picture her rolling her eyes. "There's this guy in here, he was here before. He's not doing anything weird, but I can't help thinking he is. Weird, I mean. I'm sure it's nothing..."

"I was about to come in," he interrupted. "No worries, I'll just take a look, see if he hits my weird meter too."

"Okay. I just...feel strange, making snap judgments about people like this."

"You make snap judgments about people all the time, it's natural. The question is whether or not you do anything based on those judgments. I'll be right there."

After ending the call, he pressed the speed dial for Richard's office and got voice mail, as expected. He climbed out of the car and crossed the street.

"Hey, just checking to see if you've seen anything or anyone strange today. Call me when you have a chance."

He hung up the phone and put it in his pocket as he opened the door to Grounded. He breathed in the delicious aroma and enjoyed the warm, inviting atmosphere. He spotted Taryn behind the counter immediately and made his way to her without appearing to look around.

"Guy in the blue sweater, northeast corner?" he asked her after giving her a kiss.

She glared at him. "How in the hell am I supposed to know which direction is north? He's by the hallway to the restrooms. How did you know it was him just from walking in here?"

"Because he's weird."

He had to bite his cheek to keep from laughing out loud as she actually gaped at him. He kissed her again and dragged her to her office.

Chapter Twelve

బ

Taryn was bouncing between curious and irritated and validated. Obviously she had been at least a little bit right to think there was something strange about the man in her shop, or Caleb wouldn't have known exactly who she was talking about. *Right*?

She had debated calling him for an hour before finally deciding there was no downside to making the call, other than slight embarrassment. He had told them to tell him about anything that was strange or just gave them a weird feeling and there was no question that this guy did that. So she called. And here he was.

He pulled her into her office, closing the door behind them, then paused. "Is this okay? Do you have a few minutes?"

She rolled her eyes at his tardiness in asking but smiled in pleasure that he had asked at all. He assumed correctly that meant an approval and brought her with him until he was leaning his butt against her desk and she was standing between his legs.

"Hi. Miss me?" he asked.

"Desperately," she laughed, and kissed him. She had known she couldn't keep it light so she didn't even bother trying. She practically attacked him and giggled at his surprised "oomph". She ran her hands through his hair, easily one of her favorite pastimes these days, then smacked his arm when he tried to do the same.

Pulling away from her, he narrowed his eyes. She tried to keep from laughing at him but couldn't quite manage it. His arms fell away in disgust and he just stared at her incredulously as she continued to laugh.

"Baby," she tried, but had to stop as another round of laughter hit her, more from his expression than from the original moment.

He crossed his arms over his chest. Sucking in a huge breath to calm herself, Taryn attempted her most conciliatory expression.

"Caleb, if I run my fingers through your hair it looks like you finger-combed it. If you run your fingers through my hair it looks like we just fucked on the desk."

He considered this for a moment, then relented. "It's just a theory. Maybe we should put it to a test."

"Fine. But tonight, not now. Not at work."

"You're staying with us tonight?" he asked carefully.

Sighing, Taryn turned around and leaned back against him, smiling when his arms automatically came around to hold her tight. She leaned her head against his shoulder and closed her eyes.

"Yes, I'll stay tonight. Are we still at your house? Or Richard's?"

"We have all those leftovers from Mama's in my fridge. We need to eat those."

"Okay, your house it is." He squeezed her tight then let her go, spinning her around in his arms.

"Taryn."

"Caleb."

"I like you."

She searched his face and understood. Sometimes, liking was even harder than loving. She nodded. "I like you too, a whole lot."

He gave her a quick kiss then set her away from him. "No ravishing you in your office, I assume?"

"Well, not during work hours, anyway."

He gave her a put-upon sigh. "Well then, let's talk about the guy in the blue sweater, by the bathrooms. He's been in here before?"

"The only time I've seen him was on Monday. I can ask the others if they remember seeing him before."

"Hmm. Not yet. Let's go sit at a table, see what we see."

"Okay. If we get busy though, I won't be able to stay."

"No problem."

They went out and Caleb sat at a table while Taryn made him a drink and got herself a soda. When she joined him she sat next to him, rather than across from him, so that she could see the guy too. They had only been sitting for a minute when Richard walked in.

He dropped kisses on both of their cheeks then went to the counter to order drinks for himself and his coworkers. Taryn was pretty sure the weird guy's lips pursed in disapproval, but she was afraid to stare and get a good look. She and Caleb made light chatter until Richard came and sat down while the drinks were being made up.

"How did you get stuck with delivery-boy duty today?" she asked him with a smile.

"Petra cheated. When we were giving arguments why each of us couldn't be the one to leave for a few minutes, she mentioned that she was pretty sure she'd seen Caleb walk in a little while ago, and how often did I get to see both of you in the middle of a work day?"

"So the question is, did she really see me? Or was she just lucky?" Caleb asked.

Taryn and Richard both laughed.

"Oh, she saw you, no question," said Taryn. "That woman has eyes in the back of her head. She sees all and knows all. She should have been a spy. Nobody would suspect her of a thing."

Richard nodded along with Taryn's assessment of their friend. "It's a fantastic trait in an office manager, but a little bit intimidating and occasionally frightening, too."

"Interesting," Caleb mused. "Does she have a pretty good memory for faces?"

"The best," Richard confirmed. "And names. I make her go with me every year to the big charity ball so that she can tell me who everyone is that I'm supposed to know."

Taryn was beginning to catch on. "I'll call her and ask her to come over. If Richard goes back and asks her in person she'll assume he's getting back at her for making him do the coffee run. It's sort of an ongoing battle at the office."

Richard looked confused and Caleb began to explain while Taryn used her cell phone to call Petra.

"Hey, it's Taryn. I have a huge favor. I know it's a pain, but do you think you could come over here? I swear, it's nothing to do with the coffee run and I only need you for about two minutes."

"It's important?" Petra asked.

"It is, or I swear I wouldn't call like this in the middle of the day. And seriously, I doubt it will even take the full two minutes."

"I'll be right there, but you have to send Richard back, ASAP. Mrs. Morgenstern is here and she says she's having a heart attack. You know she only listens to Richard or me."

"Will do, thanks."

"She's on her way, but you have to get back to the office. Mrs. Morgenstern is having a heart attack."

When Caleb's whole body went on alert she put her hand on his arm to reassure him. "She does this every couple of weeks, it's not a problem. She just wants to be looked at and hooked up to the machines. But Richard is always thorough, just in case."

Richard had retrieved the finished coffees while she explained to Caleb and he again kissed their cheeks before heading for the door, which Petra was holding open for him. She took her drink from the tray he was holding and joined Caleb and Taryn at their table. Caleb stood and pulled a chair out for her so that she would not have her back to the guy they were checking out. Petra gave him a startled but pleased look and took the seat.

"Hey, kids, what's up?"

Taryn leaned in and kept her voice low.

"We need to know if you recognize someone in here, but we don't want it to be obvious that you're looking."

Petra immediately became serious. "This has something to do with the vandalism?"

"Possibly. We don't really have anything to go on, we just wondered if you had any idea who the guy in the blue sweater by the bathrooms is," Caleb explained.

Leaning in even closer, Taryn whispered, "Northeast corner." She only smiled when Caleb burst out laughing. Petra at least looked like she was trying not to laugh. Taryn's abysmal sense of direction was well known.

Petra stood. "I'll just use the restroom and be right back."

Caleb waited until she had disappeared down the hallway before leaning in to kiss Taryn on the nose. She just smiled at him.

Petra reappeared quickly and they knew immediately that she had recognized the man. Her expression managed to convey both worry and sympathy. Caleb stood and Taryn realized he thought they shouldn't have this conversation in the shop. She stood too and they all walked out and headed across the street.

"I've only seen him once, at Matt Jones' funeral, a few weeks ago. That's Paul Jones, his father." Petra blurted this out in one breath, clearly concerned.

"Uh-oh," Taryn said.

"Shit," Caleb agreed. "I'm going to have one of my guys come down and keep an eye on him while I go back to the office and do some checking. If this pans out to anything, I might be pretty late tonight. This is going to seriously suck for Ricky."

"I know. I'll switch closing so I can go home with him. Call when you have an update and don't stay too late." She gave him a kiss goodbye then went with Petra to tell Richard the bad news."

Driving home after work, both she and Richard were on edge, as if the man was going to ram them in the car, despite their knowing Caleb had someone watching the guy.

Richard looked miserable and Taryn cursed to herself. It had been hard enough on him when Matt had been killed. She was certainly sympathetic to the boy's parents but none of what had happened had anything to do with Richard. He dragged his feet from the car to the house, looking morose. She pushed him into the living room and onto the couch.

Sitting next to him, she brushed his hair from his forehead and ran her other hand over his chest soothingly. "Baby, you know this has nothing to do with you. If Paul Jones is the guy who vandalized your car and house, he's obviously gone off the deep end. It's sad, yes, but not your fault. Just like what happened to Matt wasn't your fault."

"Jeez, Tare, I didn't even recognize the poor guy."

"Richard, you didn't even meet him! You saw the back of his head at the funeral service — that's about it."

He sighed and leaned his head back against the couch. Taryn had been planning on raiding the fridge for Mama's leftovers but decided that drastic cooking measures were called for to get Richard's mind off deranged fathers. She hopped up off the couch.

"Come on, let's make dinner."

"I think Caleb wanted us to eat up the leftovers."

"Too bad. Let's make him something extra yummy for having to work late." She grabbed his hand and pulled with all her weight so that he was forced not only to stand but catch her when the action nearly sent her to the ground. He didn't smile but he did follow her instructions to go change clothes. Taryn went into the kitchen and made her own special preparation.

The look on Richard's face when he walked in made being a bit uncomfortable totally worth it. She had taken off her jeans and t-shirt and was wearing only her bra, panties and an oversized apron that hung very low on her chest.

He came to her and squeezed her tight. "I'm so glad you're a part of my life."

"Yeah, whatever. What are you going to make me for dinner? I think it should involve dessert. Preferably, something with chocolate."

He swatted her on the butt. "Let's see what we have."

They opted to make chicken picatta for dinner and strawberry shortcake with chocolate sauce for dessert, since Caleb actually had fresh strawberries in the fridge.

"Do you ever wonder if Caleb appreciates the fact that he now has a well-stocked kitchen?" Richard mused, pulling out the cutting board.

"Well, if he's anything like me, mostly he appreciates that he has a well-stuffed chef." Taryn started doing what she always did when cooking with Richard. Put together the salad then sat on the counter to entertain him. She had turned the radio on, deciding it was a rock kind of night, and stopped on a station known for its eclectic mix. Aerosmith was playing and she turned it up.

"I can't believe you just said that. You want to pound the chicken breasts?"

Abandoning the tomato she was chopping, Taryn bopped her way over to where Richard had put a chicken breast into a large Ziploc bag for her. She took the offered mallet and enjoyed pounding the breast until Richard made her stop and switch to the next piece.

"I'm sorry that as your best friend I never realized that you had a problem with the whole family thing. I hope I never made you feel too uncomfortable with mine."

She paused mid-swing to look at him. "It wasn't like that, I swear. They're great, I didn't mind being near them. I just didn't want to be...well, part of them, I guess. I don't know, it's not like I was thinking, 'hey, I really like Richard but I don't want to be part of a family'. It was more unconscious, you know?"

"I still should have noticed."

Resuming her strikes, Taryn shook her head. "Hell, Rick, I barely noticed. I should be apologizing to you, not the other way around."

"Mmm-hmm, because it's all about you."

She stuck her tongue out at him.

They worked in silence for a few minutes. Richard was shuffling around, doing things with flour that she didn't pay much attention to. She switched to the last chicken breast then moved back to the tomatoes, humming along with Weezer on the radio.

The sizzling sounds of meat hitting the pan brought her to him. He angled so that she could lean in and smell the delicious scents, knowing that was one of her favorite parts of "helping" him cook. She moved back a bit so he had room to do his thing, but rested against his side.

"A lot has changed in four weeks. For both of us. For all of us, actually," he said, using the tongs to peek at the underside of the chicken.

"I wonder what he was like, as a single guy."

Richard cocked his head in thought. "That's a good question. I don't get the feeling he went out a lot, partying at least. Probably he spent a little more time at his brother's house. It's kind of weird that we never met him at the bar. I mean, we didn't go all the time, but we must have been three or four times this year."

"Maybe we weren't ready for him."

"Maybe not. I'm not sure we were ready for him four weeks ago." Richard turned the meat.

"Good point," she answered as he casually put his free arm around her before letting that hand roam her mostly naked backside. She let him play for a moment before spinning away, dancing to the Rolling Stones.

"Can't let dinner burn," she teased him.

She returned to the salad, putting the avocado pieces she had been cutting into the large bowl then tossing everything together. When she turned back he had put the chicken on a plate and was once again working with the pan. She went to set the table and called Caleb to make sure he would be home soon. He assured her that he was on his way.

Taryn hopped up on the counter to watch Richard finish the meal. He was so sexy in the kitchen, masterful but relaxed, always enjoying himself. She had seen him in doctor mode a couple of times, and while that had a high hotness factor as well, it was different. In that situation he was supremely focused on the patient, his whole being centered on what he was seeing, hearing, learning. When he cooked, it was more instinctual and much more relaxed.

"Caleb said he would be here soon, you can go ahead and plate his up, too," she told him as he turned the flame off.

"I'm glad. I hate the idea of him working late to deal with this."

"I think he enjoys it. Just like you enjoy cooking for us."

"Yeah, yeah."

Chapter Thirteen

ઔ

They worked together to get everything on the table. When it was ready, Richard reached over and switched the stereo from FM to CD. Ella Fitzgerald came on and he pulled Taryn into his arms.

Neither of them were really dancers but they could sway with the best of them. Besides, it was hard to focus on what moves to make when his arms were full of nearly naked woman. His woman. When he had walked into the kitchen and seen her like that, his heart had skipped a beat. Not only at the sexy package she presented, but knowing that she was doing it to distract him and to lift his spirits. It had certainly worked.

He let one hand drift to her ass and the other played with the hair at the nape of her neck. She leaned into him, so trusting, and he vowed not to let his insecurities damage what he had. Because they were right, he had both of them, damn it, and he wasn't going to let either one of them go.

He heard the front door open and waited until he was sure Caleb could see them before spinning around so that he was facing the hallway and Taryn's backside was presented to the other man. Taryn burrowed her face into his shoulder but he could feel her smile.

"Well. That's a lovely sight. Delicious dinner waiting on the table for a man when he gets home from a hard day at work."

They all laughed and Taryn turned in his arms. Caleb came to them and kissed first Richard, then Taryn. They stayed that way, not moving, for a whole minute before Caleb cleared his throat.

"Let's eat. Fast."

Smiling, Richard pushed Taryn toward the table.

Richard waited until they had enjoyed at least a few bites. "So?"

Caleb frowned. "So, it looks…interesting. Paul and Elsie divorced five years ago. I didn't contact her, I'd rather not until we're more sure of what's going on. She's got enough to deal with right now. I called his office and they haven't heard from him since he called and said his son was in the hospital."

"They told you that?" Taryn asked in surprise.

"Well. It's not like I just called up and asked for him. I said I was from the funeral parlor."

"Oh, right. Okay."

"My guy, Tom, followed him to a motel on the edge of town. He'll keep an eye out for any nocturnal activities. If he's our guy, I doubt it will take long for him to try to make another move, which means we'll have him. The only thing we need to do is watch him."

"It's so sad," Taryn sighed. "But I don't understand what his problem with Richard could be. Do you think it's us? Doesn't he have enough on his plate to deal with right now than to spend time worrying about what we're up to?"

Caleb nodded. "It is sad, but this kind of stress can do crazy things to a person. Maybe he's had some sort of mental meltdown. I mean, let's face it, both of us thought he was putting out a strange vibe, and really, he was just sitting there. It's entirely possible that he's not our guy and he's just coming across as so strange because of what he's going through. I'm sure there's some guilt given the fact that he doesn't live here. It sounded like he didn't spend a lot of time visiting his son."

Richard stood and began to clear the plates. "I have sympathy for the guy, but Taryn's right. I don't understand how he could fixate on me. I wasn't even working on Matt at the ER. I guess it would be different if Matt had been sick and his father thought I didn't catch it early enough, or do a proper job of treatment or something. But he was hit by a drunk driver! Why isn't he stalking that man?"

Caleb stilled, his eyes hard on Richard's. "I never actually asked what had happened. A car accident? They know who the driver was?"

Richard nodded. "Yes, it was some account exec from an advertising firm. Three DUI's on his record and he had a suspended license."

"Okay, I read about that in the paper but didn't put it together. I need to make some phone calls." Caleb stood up.

"Wait," Taryn rushed. "There's dessert."

Caleb eyed her up and down, causing Taryn to blush and Richard's heart rate to speed up.

"No! I mean, there's really dessert. Strawberry shortcake, with chocolate sauce." She rolled her eyes at both of them.

"Sounds almost perfect. Let me make one phone call, I'll be right back."

Richard let Taryn grab more dishes from the table before following her into the kitchen, so that he could watch her mostly naked body. He about ran into her when she stopped to look back at him. She quirked an eyebrow and he just grinned. Shaking her head, she began loading the dishwasher. After pulling out the dessert items, he whipped the cream and heated the chocolate sauce.

They hadn't even finished setting out the strawberries and sauce when Caleb returned. He dipped the spoon into the chocolate, letting the sweet sauce dribble back into the bowl. "Hmm. This looks...promising."

Richard cut portions of the cake for each of them and added strawberries. They worked around each other until they all had the amount of cream and sauce they wanted. Somehow, though none of them spoke or touched, eating became foreplay. Richard alternated between watching Taryn's tiny tongue dart out to catch licks of cream to Caleb's licking his fingers clean of the chocolate sauce. He might have

147

had trouble remembering to eat his own if it hadn't been so tasty.

They were nearly done when Caleb's cell phone rang.

"I'm sorry, I have to get this." He rose from the table and left the room.

Sighing, Richard made to gather the plates but Taryn stopped him.

"I'll get these, why don't you go into the living room, he probably won't be long. I'm sure we won't have any trouble getting him back on track."

He kissed her fingers. "Thanks, sweetie."

In the living room, he collapsed on the overstuffed couch he never would have picked for its style, though he couldn't deny its comfort. Closing his eyes, he imagined what a living room decorated for the three of them would be like. While he was very style conscious, he was also a believer in making a room fit its inhabitants. That could be a challenge sometimes, depending on current styles, which only made things more fun.

Smiling to himself as he imagined Taryn's reaction to the idea that decorating was fun, he populated a large but imaginary room in a way that would suit their three distinct personalities. It had to be a made-up room, he mused, as none of their current houses would work for all three of them. Best if they all started somewhere new together.

As if it were already decided. Hell, just yesterday he had been convinced they were going to dump him and get married, and now he was ready to make a home with them.

Caleb came in holding his car keys, with Taryn just behind him. He sat down on the edge of the coffee table, his look very serious. "The call was the answer I was waiting for, but also an emergency with one of my clients. I have to go deal with that." He shook his head. "The timing sucks, because the answer to my question wasn't good." Taking a deep breath, he reached a hand out to Richard.

"The bastard who hit Matt Jones, Louis Arnold, is dead. He was knifed in the county lockup last week."

Richard wasn't sure if he should feel happy or sad, pity or relief. Mostly he just felt numb. "You think Mr. Jones arranged it somehow."

"It's a possibility I think we should raise with your sister. Laura can get the info to the right people. They may even be looking for him, to ask him some questions. He would be an obvious suspect, but they might not know where he is."

"He wasn't exactly hiding at my shop," Taryn pointed out.

"True, but I doubt he guessed anybody would recognize him. At any rate, it can't hurt to give the cops a heads-up. I've sent a second operative to stay with him, make sure we don't lose him. I should be back in a few hours. I'm hoping you guys will stay inside."

Richard laughed at Caleb's obvious attempt to not tell them what to do and piss Taryn off again. "I seriously doubt we'll have any desire to leave the house before morning, but if we do, we'll call you."

Caleb stood and so did Richard and Taryn.

"What you're doing tonight, it's not dangerous is it?" Taryn asked.

"Not at all. Just corporate hand holding." He kissed them both goodbye and Richard set the alarm behind him.

They returned to the living room and he flopped down onto the large chair, pulling Taryn down onto his lap. She snuggled in close, resting one hand above his shirt collar, her thumb tracing his collarbone. The sweet smell of her warm skin surrounded him and he drew in a deep lungful.

"Sweetie, this apron's not quite soft enough for your skin. It's probably irritating. Why don't I help you take it off?"

A smirk was her first response. Turning to present the tie at the back of her neck was her second. The ties were quickly undone and he unclasped her bra while it was handy. His hands caressed her shoulders as lightly as he could manage, pushing the bra straps down and causing goose bumps to pebble on her skin.

She was a vision, wearing only her panties while seated on his jeans-covered lap. He reached a hand out and used one finger to trace her cheekbones, her chin, her nose. She narrowed her eyes at him but he ignored that and let his eyes show her what he was feeling. Her teasing expression fell away and she closed her eyes, just long enough for him to get nervous. When they opened, they were shiny with unshed tears and his heart skipped a beat. Already beautiful, the love and vulnerability so clear on her face transformed her into extraordinary.

"Sometimes, when we're walking down the street together, you'll catch a man's eye. You're completely oblivious but I'll watch him turn to take a second look, watch his eyes rake you up and down, watch his pants bulge. Watch his irritation as he realizes you're with me. I think it's the only time I ever feel arrogant. That this beautiful woman is with me, and they're just out of luck."

She blinked and one of the tears fell. He leaned in and traced its path with his tongue, ending at the corner of her mouth. She opened her mouth to respond but he stopped her with a kiss. He explored her in a way he hadn't done in months, maybe even longer. He explored her like he didn't already know how wonderful she tasted, the fascinating textures that she was made of. After a time he pulled back and rested his forehead against hers.

At some point his hands had found her breasts and they squeezed gently, caressing the round globes but neglecting the tight points until she whispered, so softly, "Please."

He took both nipples between thumbs and forefingers and pulled, giving a sharp pinch. She cried out and launched into her own action. Her hands tore at his t-shirt, trying to get it over his head despite the fact that he was now lowering his head to one nipple and sucking it in, hard. She gave up on his t-shirt with a cry, her fingers going to work on his belt instead. She froze when he switched to her other peak, then resumed with a frantic groan.

"Ricky." Her desperation made him soar.

"Taryn." He whispered it, a benediction.

When she jerked his fly open and reached inside he was so thankful he had chosen to go commando tonight. He'd had a vague thought about checking out Caleb's reaction but now all he could think was *thankyouthankyouthankyou.*

He barely had the presence of mind to let her go long enough to reach into the drawer in the table between the chair and the sofa and hand her a condom, before returning his hands to their treasures. He pushed her breasts together and tongued the peaks simultaneously. Her delicate hands fumbled to pull him out of his jeans and put the condom on. He helped her rise up and position her legs to either side of his, then stared into her eyes as she lowered, sliding home.

Aaaahhhh. He couldn't think, couldn't plan, could only revel in the glorious sensation of hot, wet Taryn gripping him so tightly. Bracing his elbows against the chair arms, he held her waist and pulled her up while easing back. They watched each other's eyes as he slowly brought her back down, hips rising to meet her.

"Taryn." He tried to tell her everything, tell her how much she meant to him, how much he loved her, but all that he could manage was her name.

"Richard." It started out a whisper but ended on a gasp as he thrust into her again.

Losing the ability to pace himself, Richard urged her to ride him hard, and she did. He took one hand from her hip and sifted through her curls to find her clit. She jerked and leaned over to brace her hands against his shoulders. He wanted to see her come, wanted to watch the pleasure overtake her while he could still pay attention. He pinched the small bundle of nerves then massaged it.

Her head fell back, her mouth open on a silent scream as her hips stilled, her inner muscles clenching and unclenching him in climax. It was almost impossible but he held back, determined to watch her to the end. Her eyes were closed, her breathing harsh and she had never looked more beautiful. Finally she opened her eyes and looked at him, her smile supremely satisfied before it turned wicked. She clenched her muscles tightly, everywhere, thighs, arms, pussy, and ground herself against him. The surge overtook him in a heartbeat, his balls emptying out in a rush that seemed to last forever.

Sighing, she draped herself over him and went boneless. He clutched her close and fell asleep.

Chapter Fourteen

ഇ

Caleb saw that the lights were still on when he got home, so he wasn't particularly quiet coming into the house. He assumed they were still talking in the living room or watching television. Despite the noise he had made, they were fast asleep when he spotted them on the large chair in the living room. Richard appeared to still be dressed but Taryn had lost her apron and underwear. She was draped over him, his arms tight around her.

He watched them for a few minutes. They were part of his life now and he had never been happier, despite the craziness of the last couple days. He wanted to ask them to move in with him, to his parents' old house, but he wasn't sure they were ready and didn't want to scare them. Used to being confident, his uncertainty was maddening. They were obviously tired and he debated waking them up only long enough to shuffle them off to bed versus taking the time and pleasure to remind them that they belonged to him now, just as much as he belonged to them.

"Taryn. Ricky."

Taryn stirred, stretching her naked body against Richard as she yawned and blinked up at Caleb. Oh yeah, there was no need to struggle with the decision, it was clearly time to remind them that in one thing, at least, he was in charge.

"Taryn. Stand up." His voice was even and firm. She responded to it instantly, her breath picking up, her nipples beading. She carefully got out of Richard's lap and stood next to the chair, her eyes glued to him.

"Richard." He scanned the other man's face, relieved to see that much of the exhaustion he'd seen at dinner was gone. Now Richard looked sleepy but ready. "Stand up."

Complying, Richard stood next to Taryn. He was fully dressed except for his dick hanging out of his pants. Caleb saw a used condom in a Kleenex on the table by the chair. He ran through a nearly endless list of possibilities on what he wanted to do next. He considered using the cuffs but decided that for tonight he wanted them following directions without the benefit of restraints.

"Ricky, take off your clothes." Taryn jerked as if she was going to help him but her hands stayed at her sides as Richard hurriedly undressed. Caleb took his time undressing, not matching the other man's pace. They waited, silently, while he finished.

"Richard, will you get the down comforter from the linen closet? It's on the top shelf, and get one of the blankets, too. Taryn, help me slide the couch back a bit."

When he had the comforter, Caleb spread it over the wide coffee table, doubling the comforter up, then covering it with the soft blanket. It was a wood coffee table, with drawers underneath, very solid, about knee high. With the couch pushed back he could easily walk around it.

"Taryn, get on the table, on your knees." Her eyes darted to his, then Richard's, as she made her way to the table and slowly climbed on. She knelt back on her heels but he shook his head at her and she rose up to her full kneeling height.

"Richard, on your knees, too, behind her. I want your legs bracketing hers." Richard did as he was told, holding Taryn's shoulders carefully while he balanced himself as Caleb wanted him. "Get in tight, I want you almost touching her back." His voice was getting rough but he fought to keep it even. Taryn and Richard were both breathing harder, unsure of what he was going to do.

"Now, don't move unless I tell you to," he reminded them.

Centered as they were, there were only a couple of inches of table left on either side of them. Caleb was able to stand next to them, and touch them easily. He brought his left hand up Richard's thigh, over his buttock, the dip of his waist. He spread his hand wide to fully appreciate the muscles of the back, smoothing his hand up the shoulder blade, sliding in slightly until he could cup the nape of his neck. He squeezed gently and Richard's eyes closed.

He used his right hand to follow a similar path, up Taryn's thigh, tickling through the crease where thigh meets hip, over the slightly rounded stomach, hand spreading wide to cup the breast for only a second before sliding over the begging nipple and farther up to curve along her shoulder and in, until he was cupping her neck, his thumb caressing her jaw, his fingers loosely about her throat.

Both of them trembled under his hold, ever so slightly, but they remained still. "Mine." Taryn swallowed hard under his hand. He ran his fingers through her hair, twisting the mass into a rope he draped over her shoulder so that he could see both of their faces.

Nipping Taryn's shoulder blade, he nibbled his way up to her earlobe. She started to turn her head, to meet him, but he stopped her with a hand on her chin and she resumed her position. He let the hand fall away as he kissed and licked and nipped his way around her chin to the corner of her mouth. "Don't move," he reminded her, the barest of whispers just above her lips. She made a tiny sound of distress, probably without even noticing it. He licked her lips, already parted for her panting breaths, but she stayed still. He breathed her in, nuzzled her nose with his own while he brought his right hand to the juncture of her thighs.

He knew she could feel the heat of his hand, so close but not actually touching. He swore he could feel her own heat and moisture, begging for him to touch her. With his mouth, he worked his way back to ear and sucked the earlobe in hard while he tested her readiness. She was wet and getting wetter. He cupped her gently at first, then firmly, pleased when she resisted rocking into his hold. "Mine," he whispered again, directly into her ear. "Tell me."

"Yes, Caleb. Yours."

He removed his hand slowly and turned to Richard. "You're being so good, both of you. Is it hard, Rick? What would you do now, if you could?"

"Sli-slide into her."

"Is that right?" Caleb asked, licking Richard's shoulder. "But you're not going to, are you?"

Richard swallowed. "No, Caleb."

Caleb gave him a small bite then soothed the spot with kisses. He worked his way down to Richard's nipple and took it between his fingers, tweaking it while he sucked gently on the hollow of Richard's throat, then teased his lips as he had done Taryn's. He pulled the full lower lip between his teeth, letting it go with a pop.

Resting his forehead against Richard's temple, he eased his hand down between their bodies to find the hard arousal waiting for him. The cock pulsed hot in his hand, jerking slightly at his touch. He rubbed the tip against Taryn's backside, the pre-cum sliding along where their skin made contact. Richard gasped and he squeezed in warning. "Mine," he whispered again. Richard shuddered but said nothing. Caleb leaned in so that Richard could feel the smile against his cheek, feel the words against his jaw. "Tell me."

"Yes, Caleb, yours."

Letting go, Caleb walked around the table, using just one finger to trail along their bodies. He traced nipples and biceps, ears and elbows, using only the one finger as he circled them. They were beautiful. They were his. Stopping at their side, he once again captured Richard's cock and cupped Taryn's pussy.

"You'll move when I tell you to move."

"Yes, Caleb," they both answered.

"You'll stop when I tell you to stop."

"Yes, Caleb."

He stepped away and pulled a condom from the small table drawer. He held it out to Richard. "Put it on." While Richard did so he moved to the overstuffed chair and sat down. It was perfectly positioned so that he could see them both, see where they came together, or would, in a minute. When Richard had returned his hands to his side, Caleb spoke.

"Taryn, I want your face flat on your hands, looking at me." She lowered herself down, elbows bent to the side, hips high in the air.

"Richard, she's ready for you. Fill her up." Richard glanced at him in slight panic. "You can use your hands."

With one hand on her hip, he used the other to guide himself in, one long, slow movement. Taryn sighed and Richard let out the breath he had been holding.

"Now stop." Though they hadn't actually been moving at that point, they both somehow stilled further, frozen. "Look at me, Richard."

Chocolate-brown eyes turned to him, burning with need. Caleb let them both see his desire for them, his appreciation for what he was seeing. He slowly stroked his own shaft while his eyes roamed the pair. They clearly strained to remain still, melded from knee to groin, Richard's olive hands steady on Taryn's pale hips.

He increased his pressure, then his pace, imagining Taryn's wet pussy holding him tight, imagining Richard's tongue working him like a popsicle.

"From the moment I saw you, I wanted you both. Give him a squeeze, Taryn, one good one. I wanted you both because you looked so good together, and then I talked to you." Sweat dripped down Richard's temple, his hand slippery on Taryn's slick hip. They were both breathing faster, eyes becoming desperate the more he spoke.

"The more I got to know you, the more sure I was that you were mine. The more time we spent together, the harder it was to imagine my future without you both." His hand picked up speed once more and his speech became a little rougher.

"I know that if you tell me that you can't be with me, I'll have to let you go, but you would take a part of me with you. I don't think I told you before, but I've never said 'I love you' to any other lover. Ever." He paused for a couple of beats. "Richard, in and out, just once, nice and slow."

Groaning, Richard did as he was told. Taryn's eyes squeezed shut, but only for a second, opening again before he could tell her.

"I want to go to sleep to the sound of your breathing every night and wake up in the tangle of your arms and legs every morning." He squeezed just under the head tightly before continuing. He pumped hard now, their eyes locked to his hand on his dick, his hips meeting his own thrusts. He could see Taryn's juices running down both of their thighs.

He came, hard and fast, splashing his release onto his stomach. "Don't move, either of you." He could see the desperation on their faces, knew it was time, knew they were barely holding on. "Come, now."

Without any further movement, they both shouted as they came. Richard fell over Taryn, elbows locked to hold himself off her. Caleb stood and knelt beside them. He kissed Richard, then Taryn. "Thank you. That was beautiful."

He helped Richard up off the table while Taryn let her legs fold underneath her. Richard hobbled a bit but managed most of his weight as Caleb led him to the bathroom, then the bed. Returning to the living room, he scooped Taryn up and brought her to Richard's side. He left them only long enough to turn off all the lights and double-check the security alarm, then he climbed onto the bed and snuggled in tight before falling asleep.

* * * * *

The phone rang much too early and Caleb knew it couldn't be good news. Richard was immediately awake, and being closest to the phone, he answered before the second ring. Despite his foreboding, Caleb nearly laughed when, after barking hello, Richard suddenly realized it wasn't his own phone he was holding. He grimaced a sheepish apology to Caleb and cleared his throat. "Yeah, he's right here." He handed the phone over and Caleb smiled his reassurance.

"Yes."

"It's Diana. The subject left his motel room a few minutes ago. I think he's headed to your house. At least that's the direction he's going right now."

Caleb stood up and motioned to the others to get up as well. "How far away are you?"

"If he goes straight to your house, about seven to ten minutes."

With the phone tucked between his shoulder and his ear, he pulled on his jeans. "I'm going to call the police, ask them to send a patrol this way." He hung up and pulled on a t-shirt. The worried expression on Richard's face reminded him to keep his cool.

"Paul Jones left the motel a few minutes ago and my operatives think he might be headed this way. I just want us dressed and prepared, that's all. I think it's better if the police handle it. That way, even if he doesn't start anything, they can just ask him to move on." He paused to dial the phone. "If he does try something, then they can witness it and deal with it rather then get into a he said/she said situation. Even with witnesses, you shouldn't have to defend your actions. We'll stay inside, see what happens."

Richard picked up his cell phone. "I'll call Laura, too, see if she's on duty."

They made their respective calls, then hung up.

"They're sending a car," Caleb said.

"Laura's off duty, but is going to come by anyway." Richard studied Caleb's face. "You're staying inside with us because you know we won't stay if you don't. But you'd rather go out there yourself."

"Shit yeah. But it's not the smart plan for me either. Maybe in my younger days, I would have anyway, but this is your reputation at stake here, I'll take smart over action, no matter how fun it might be."

Nodding his head, Richard finished getting dressed. Taryn gave him a kiss on the cheek and headed down the hall. Knowing her, she was probably putting on coffee. That worked out well, since he had already determined the kitchen was the safest place to put them until he knew what was happening.

Richard paced while Taryn pulled out mugs, sugar and cream.

Caleb tried to reassure him. "It's going to be fine. This is why we had a team on him, so there wouldn't be any surprises." Richard just nodded and Taryn sat down, then jumped when the phone rang.

"Yes," Caleb answered.

"It's Diana, he's still headed your way. I would say there's little doubt."

"Fine, hang back, I don't want him getting nervous. There will be a patrol car here in a couple of minutes. They know you're following so they shouldn't bother you." He hung up and turned off the light in the kitchen. He'd left a light on in the bedroom so they had enough spilling down the hall to see, but wouldn't themselves be visible through the windows.

"He's almost here. Stay in the kitchen and I'll take a look, see what's going on."

Taryn actually laughed at him and Richard just shook his head.

They started out of the kitchen but he stepped in front of them. "Richard. Taryn. Let me do this. Please." He wished he could just order them but that didn't seem to be working so well. "This is what I do."

"Caleb, he spray painted my house, but there's no reason to think we're in danger watching out a window."

"He also knifed your tires and might be responsible for the death of his son's killer." Aggravated, he ran his hand through his hair and sighed. "How about if you stand just inside the living room. You can still see out when I open the curtain a bit, but you can be back in the kitchen in one step."

"Sure," Taryn agreed, "if you stay with us. Or give us a good reason why it's more dangerous for us than it is for you."

"Because I know when to duck." He raised his hands against further protests. "Fine, I'll stay back here with you." Clearly it was the only way he was going to be able to make sure they stayed out of trouble.

They both nodded and he went to the curtain, peeking out to make sure there was no activity on the street, then opening it just enough that they could see from the back of the room.

They stood in silence for a couple of minutes before a pair of headlights turned the corner at the far end of the street. The car slowed then stopped in front of the house. The headlights turned off and nothing else happened. The nearest street light was close enough that they could just barely make out someone sitting in the driver's seat, but nothing more.

The phone rang and this time it was Richard who jumped. He laughed ruefully at himself while Caleb answered.

"Yes."

"We're just around the corner, but we have a good visual. The patrol car is just about to pass us."

"Thanks." Hanging up, he relayed the information to the others as they all watched another set of headlights turn the corner. The patrol car approached the parked car and stopped just behind it. Two uniformed officers got out and made their way up either side of the car. The patrolman on the driver's side directed his flashlight at the driver.

In an instant both officers pulled their guns. Caleb opened his mouth to order Taryn and Richard back into the kitchen then shut it. They would never listen to him if he kept telling them to do things that weren't yet necessary. He had to bite his tongue but he kept silent.

"Put your hands on the wheel." They could just make out the words from the street. "On the wheel!" The officer on the driver's side shouted while the other cop tried the passenger side door and opened it. He reached in and came out holding a gun.

The first officer opened the driver's door. "Out of the car and on the ground, now!"

The man stumbled out of the car and fell to the pavement, sobbing. The officers quickly had him handcuffed and in the backseat of their car. One of them stayed with the car while the other approached the house. Taryn and Richard both looked shaken but they all moved toward the door. As he opened it, Caleb saw Laura drive up.

"We might as well wait for Officer Daniels. She'll want to hear this, too," Caleb said, shaking hands with the man who introduced himself as Officer Morales.

"There's coffee if you'd like to come in," Taryn offered, her voice unsteady.

She had a cup ready for Laura as the woman walked in, taking it with a grateful sigh.

"So what happened?" she asked, directing her question to Officer Morales.

"We approached the subject sitting in his car. When we got close enough, we saw he was holding a revolver. He didn't seem to be aware of our approach until I called out to him. He was fixated on this house. Officer Tucker was able to secure the gun and the subject was handcuffed. We searched the subject and he had no other weapons and no identification, let alone a gun permit. He was unresponsive when questioned, other than incoherent babbling. Officer Tucker is searching the car."

"I'd like to see if these guys recognize him." Laura gestured to the group and Officer Morales nodded, grabbing a fresh cup of coffee for his partner then leading the way outside.

Officer Tucker took the offered mug. "There was a vandalism incident? With spray paint?" he asked.

"That's right, at my house," Richard confirmed.

"Well, there is spray paint in the trunk. Red."

They moved closer to the squad car. Caleb nodded. "That's the man we saw at Taryn's coffee shop yesterday, who was identified to us as Paul Jones."

"So, that's it then, right? He's the guy?" Richard asked. "I just don't get it. I didn't do anything to him."

"Probably he's the guy," Laura said. "Definitely, he's going to jail. They'll take him down to the station, see if they can get anything out of him." She turned to Officer Morales. "You'll want to let Detective O'Reilly know. He's looking for Paul Jones for questioning about a murder case."

Morales nodded and moved off, pulling out his radio.

"Well," Taryn pointed out. "That was briefly frightening but mostly anticlimactic."

"That's the way we like it." Caleb gestured them back into the house. He watched them closely. Richard seemed sad and Taryn a little shaky. She really had underestimated the danger and he was glad to see she was finally realizing how serious the situation had been.

Chapter Fifteen

ဢ

"I'm going to take a shower," Taryn announced as soon as they walked back into the house. "I might as well go into the shop early."

She didn't wait for a response. She showered and dressed in record time, refusing to slow down enough to let her brain work. She didn't want to think about what had just happened. Or what could have just happened. Moving quickly, she gathered her purse from the living room and stuck her head into the kitchen where Caleb and Richard were offering more coffee to the officers. "Off to work, see you later." She was out the door before they had a chance to respond, as long as she didn't take Caleb's eyes narrowing dangerously at her or Richard's look of surprise as a response.

She had to enter the code on the alarm twice to get it right. Finally, she was able to open the door to the coffee shop. She shut it behind her and went straight to her office, moving quickly. The door closed with a soft click and she leaned against it. Space, her space. She had been spending too many nights at Caleb's house, she needed some time to herself.

Dropping her purse on her desk, she sat heavily in the chair, angrily pushing the power button on her computer monitor. Remembering the looks on Caleb and Richard's faces as she'd left, she scowled. They had to understand that she wasn't used to spending 24/7 with other people, even people she loved. It was perfectly normal to want some space and time to herself, right?

They should respect her right to privacy, damn it. The phone rang and her irritation intensified, knowing it was one of them. She snatched it up.

"What?" she asked, barely managing to keep from shouting.

"Taryn? This is Claudia, are you okay?"

"Oh." Oh shit. Her paper products distributer was in a different time zone and frequently left her messages early in the morning. "I'm so sorry, Claudia, can I call you back in a little while?"

"Of course, I never expected you to answer in the first place. I'll talk to you later."

"Thanks, Claudia."

The phone hit the cradle with a loud click. Taryn's head hit the desk with a dull thud. What was wrong with her? Why couldn't she just be happy? She finally had everything she'd ever wanted – the perfect guy *and* Richard, who had become even more important to her than before. She had...she had family. Groaning, she thunked her head again. Family. She had to give Caleb credit, he was pretty smart to have hit on that little issue as quickly as he had. She'd never even admitted to herself how much the idea terrified her.

I mean, really. Was it worth the risk? Look how close they had come to disaster this morning. If Paul Jones hadn't been stopped before Richard walked out the door this morning... If he had pulled out his gun...

She shuddered and her head swam as all the blood drained from her face. Richard could have been shot, or even Caleb. Caleb probably would have tried to race in front of the bullet to save Richard. They would both get shot but Caleb would stop the asshole before he shot Taryn. And then where would she be? Standing there, with both of them shot. Both of them dead. And her alone. Again.

She picked up her stapler and threw it against the wall. It made a satisfying crack so she tried the tape dispenser. Suddenly the door burst open and she screamed, grabbing the phone to throw next.

Caleb and Richard stood there, eyes darting around the office.

"What? For fuck's sake, what?" She was nearly shouting but couldn't seem to stop herself. "Can't I spend just a few minutes by myself without you breaking into my shop and busting down my damn door?"

Richard's eyes were wide in astonishment and Caleb's soft with pity. The blood returned to her face in a boiling rage. Pity? What the hell did he have to pity her for? She had a fantastic business, an adorable apartment, and regular sex with two sexy men. She did not need his pity.

Forcing her voice to a normal level, she didn't wait for them to respond. "I'm trying to run a business here, if you two don't mind."

"You have cockroaches?" Caleb asked evenly.

"What!? Of course not, how could you say that? I do not have cockroaches!" Damn it, now she was yelling again.

"I figured that's what you were throwing the office equipment at." He used his foot to nudge the stapler lying on its side.

"That is not funny."

"Neither is you running away," Richard said quietly.

"I am not running away. I am working."

"You don't open for another two hours," Caleb reminded her.

"I don't tell you how to run your business, you stay out of mine."

Caleb nodded, took a step forward. "I can do that, but this has nothing to do with business."

Her throat was getting tight and it was getting harder to breathe. Shit, what was wrong with her? She needed them to leave so she could think.

Richard took two steps forward and Caleb another. She didn't want them here, didn't want them to touch her.

"Go away." She barely managed a whisper around the lump in her throat.

They separated, one coming around each side of the desk. She eyed the desk to see if she could cross over without killing her computer. Before she had a chance to decide, they were too close.

"Go away," she tried again, but this time she actually croaked. Shit, shit, shit. She was not going to cry. There was nothing to cry about, damn it. Everyone was safe. Nobody was shot. Nobody was dead. They were still here. She just needed them to go away.

Caleb pulled her in tight, her back to his chest, and Richard moved in to hug her from the front. She remained stiff. They would take the hint, not to mention the outright orders, and leave, as long as she didn't respond.

"I don't want you here," she tried again.

"Here, at the shop? Or here, hugging you? Or here, in your life?" Richard asked. He lifted her chin, tilting her head back until it rested against Caleb's chest and he could see her face clearly.

"We don't have to be together every minute. Or every day."

"No?" Caleb asked. "So how much time do we need to spend together to be just friends with benefits? When does it edge into lovers? Are we lovers, Taryn? Or are we in a relationship? How many hours equals a relationship? Is that the edge we're drawing too near? Or are we past that and heading at warp speed toward family? How many hours a week do we have to spend together to be a family?"

His breath caressed her ear as he spoke softly. She could hear the steel in his voice but his hands were gentle on her arms.

"Are we a family now, Taryn?" Richard picked up. "Is that what you're running from? Because some stupid piece of shit threatened us, you're going to give this up?"

"I didn't say...I don't...It's not..." She couldn't breathe, couldn't think, couldn't speak. She pushed at Richard but that just brought her closer to Caleb. She tried to pull back but Richard stepped impossibly closer.

"Please, please leave me alone. I want to be alone." Horrified, she felt a tear escape. She hated to cry, never did. At least, not before she'd met Caleb. Somehow this was all his fault.

"You're not alone, not anymore." Caleb's voice broke and she was so surprised she tried to look back at him but he wouldn't let her move. "You have us now, whether you want to admit it or not. We're not going anywhere. We love you."

"That's stalking," she hiccupped. "I'll call the cops."

She heard him sigh as his chin dropped to rest on her head. She brought her eyes up to Richard's and her heart broke at the pain she saw there. A tiny whimper escaped. She hadn't done that, had she? She didn't want to hurt him, them. She just needed some time to herself, was that too much to ask? She tried to explain, tried to make them understand, but the words wouldn't come. The tears were flowing freely now so it took her a minute to realize that Richard was crying, too.

"No," she sobbed. "Don't cry. Please, Richard." Her voice was rough, cracked. He just shook his head at her.

"Don't you understand how much we hate to see you in pain? How much we hate that our love hurts you?" he asked.

"It doesn't!" she cried. "I love..." She tried to take a breath. "I love you both, so much."

"Then don't you see?" Caleb asked, his voice sounding desperate. "It's already too late. It will already hurt if we die. So why not take what you can get. If we both died tomorrow, wouldn't you rather have loved us today than run from us?"

Whatever tiny shred was holding her together to that point dissolved and she would have collapsed if they weren't propping her up. Caleb scooped her into his arms, following Richard out of her office and to the door leading to her apartment. Richard had a key and he used it now while she tried to gather herself back together, tried to stop crying, to figure out what she needed to do to get them to leave. She needed to regroup, figure out how to make them...how to keep them from being so important...how to love them a little less.

Fuck. *Fuckfuckfuckfuck.* "I can't...I ca-can't..." She was gasping so hard she could feel Caleb struggling to hold onto her as he climbed the stairs to her apartment, but she couldn't stop.

"Shhh, baby, don't try to talk, you need to calm down, just a little bit, just so you can breathe."

"But...I can't..."

Richard unlocked the door and led the way to her bedroom. He sat on the bed and Caleb deposited her into his arms.

"Shush, sweetie, breathe. You're going to make yourself sick."

Caleb came back with a wet washcloth and tried to wipe her face. She batted him away but was breathing a little better.

"I can't love you this much. Please, Caleb, please, not this much. It hurts too much to be alone."

"I know, baby, you don't want to be alone."

"Right. No. No, I don't want to love you. Not this much."

"Because then it will hurt when you're alone. So you'd rather be alone now."

"No, no, that's not what I'm saying!"

"Okay," Richard soothed. "Okay, we can talk about this later. Why don't you close your eyes, get a little more sleep."

"I have to work."

"I thought you said Emma was opening for you today?"

"You have to work."

"What's that got to do with your getting some sleep?"

She wrinkled her brow, confused. "But…"

Caleb leaned in, kissed her forehead. "Shh, baby, just close your eyes."

She huffed, sure he was being unreasonably demanding, but unable to figure out how or why just now. Her eyes hurt anyway, since the jerks had made her cry, so she closed them. Richard scooted down a bit so they were lying more fully on the bed and the cool washcloth settled over her eyelids, feeling heavenly.

She had no idea how much time had passed when she woke. All three of them were in her bed and she was wearing just her t-shirt and underpants. She took a minute to wonder if they had taken off her shirt, then her bra, then put the shirt back on, or if they had managed to remove the bra without taking the shirt off.

She must have moved because Caleb propped his head up on his arm so that he could look at her.

"Hi," was all he said.

She couldn't meet his eyes or stop the blush from creeping up her neck.

"Hi. I'm sorry."

"Are you?" she heard Richard ask from behind her.

"Yes." She rolled over so that she was on her back, staring at the ceiling.

"But do you still feel the same way?" Caleb asked.

"Yes. I don't know. Maybe."

"Oh well. Okay then." Richard's wry response wrung a small smile from her before she sighed and closed her eyes.

"Everything changed when they died. My whole world…changed."

She kept her eyes closed, listened to them breathing, waiting.

"I know it's ridiculous that something that happened so long ago is still screwing me—" She stopped when a finger crossed her lips.

Startled, she opened her eyes and found Caleb above her, frowning.

"I want you to tell us without putting yourself down." He quirked an eyebrow. "Think you can manage that?"

She rolled her eyes at him to keep the sheepish expression off her face. "Fine. They died. Were killed, actually. Did I tell you it was a train accident?" She tried to remember but gave up. "I used to use that word—accident—but mostly now I say they were killed. It sure as hell wasn't an accident."

She sat up and rearranged herself more comfortably against the headboard.

"This...man parked his car on the tracks when he knew the commuter train was coming. He wanted to die. Nobody knows what thought he gave to the people on the train. If he was just an ignorant asshole or if he wanted to take as many people with him as he could. His wife had just left him, you see. She was tired of his cheating on her and spending all of their money. So she left him and took their daughter with her."

"Did you know all of this at the time?" Caleb asked.

"Oh sure. It was on all the news and everyone at school was talking about it. Everyone knew. I always wondered what it was like for his daughter. She was seven." Richard moved so that he was facing her and took her hand in his. She stared at that, at their hands clasped together, before forcing herself to go on.

"The funeral was awful. The guardian my parents had chosen didn't want me. My grandmother was a drunk. She didn't want me either, but they basically bribed her to take me, so she did. I spent the next few years pretty much trying to hide the fact that she was a drunk because I figured living with her was better than some sort of facility or unknown foster care home." She stopped, shook her head. "I need something to drink."

They trooped off to her tiny kitchen and she got a bottle of water. Turning to ask the guys if they wanted anything, she caught their looks of surprise. "You thought I meant alcohol? I'm not averse to it, as you know, but it's for when I want to have a good time with friends, not drown my sorrows."

They went to the couch and Caleb pulled her onto his lap, resting his chin on her head, as he liked to do. She felt so safe and comfortable, she couldn't exactly remember why she had run from this.

"One day my grandmother went grocery shopping while I was at school. I have no idea why, since I always did the shopping, but she was drunk. She made a scene at the store and then hit a car in the parking lot. My aunt came over from Colorado and put her in a nursing facility and took me back with her. She was mostly fine as long as I didn't bother her and stayed in the spare room whenever her friends came over."

"Male friends?" Richard asked.

"Yes, but also her regular friends. She liked to party. I bet most of them never even knew I was there. The day I turned eighteen I left. Stayed with a couple of friends until graduation then went back to California for college. You know the rest."

"Why did you go back to California? It would have been cheaper to do college in Colorado, where you had residency, right?"

"I had enough money and there was no reason to stay."

"You had that little apartment, and were never frivolous with your money, but you would have saved more if you'd taken a dorm or shared an apartment. But you never had roommates," Richard commented.

"I needed my own space."

"Yes, you did. Do you still?"

She swallowed hard and Caleb's arms tightened around her. "I don't know. I thought I did. This morning, I needed it."

"But not because we were crowding you," Caleb pointed out. "So why this morning? Why so soon after they took him away? You didn't even wait until all of the cops were gone."

She tried to sit up but he held her close. "Tell us."

"He could have killed you." She spat the words out like they tasted nasty on her tongue.

"He could have killed you, too. But he didn't. We stayed safe and smart and no one was hurt."

"He had a gun and he could have killed you. Either one of you. Both of you."

"And then you would have lost us. What difference does it make, though, to have us if you don't want to be with us?" Richard asked.

"I never said I didn't want to be with you!"

"You told us to go away and leave you alone."

"Not forever!" She was verging on the very edge of mad again but couldn't quite summon the energy.

"No, just when you needed us."

Her shoulders slumped in defeat. She couldn't exactly argue. What the hell was wrong with her?

"I went to their house—once." She didn't know she was going to say the words until they were already said.

"Whose house, baby?" Caleb's rational voice from a minute ago was replaced by one of compassion.

"The meant-to-be guardian's. Her name was Megan, but I always think of her as The Guardian."

"What did you find?" Richard asked.

"Two happy people with two happy children. And a dog. Nice cars, little league."

"Did you talk to them?"

"No. I just watched. One whole day, from the park across the street. Can you believe it? A park, right across the street."

"I'm sorry," Caleb said. "She should have cared. They both should have."

"I'm sure she thought she did. I'm sure they convinced themselves they were doing the best thing for their family. They were right to make their own kids their priority."

"What they did was wrong, plain and simple," Richard disagreed. "Did they ever even check on you, to see how things were going?"

"Not that I know of."

"What was their last name again?" Caleb asked, his voice playfully menacing. At least, she hoped it was playful.

Richard looked down at the bed, then back up, looking almost...shy. She reached out, took his hand.

"Do you think..." He shook his head, opened his mouth again, then closed it, before giving a forced chuckle. "Never mind.

"Richard." She couldn't stand to see him like this, wanted to smack herself for causing this when he'd already had a shitty day.

Caleb reached out too, resting his hand on Richard's arm. "Tell us."

"It's stupid, I was just...well, I was just wondering if this is why you stayed with me for so long." He ducked his head again and she tried to pull him closer but he was already there.

"What do you mean?"

"You know, because I wasn't any threat to being permanent. I was just, you know, a lover. Not a boyfriend. Not potential family."

Pulling her hand back, she glared at him. "I loved you. Not like I do now, sure, but you didn't think of me like that, either."

"I know, you're right." He shook his head, grimacing. "It's stupid, to look back on how things were, when as great as it was, it didn't come close to what we have now."

Caleb nuzzled her hair as he brought his hand down Richard's arm to entwine their fingers. "I think you asked it in a...well, not brilliant way, but you're partially right. She wasn't ready for that, for home and family, but then neither were you. At least, not with her. But you were able to give each other so much love and happiness while you waited and grew and..." He paused as if unsure how to finish.

"Waited for you?" Taryn asked with a smile.

"Well, yeah. I'm hard to resist."

She gave him as much of a laugh as she could. She didn't want to be sad anymore, or angry. Or alone. "I have no idea what time it is, or if I should be at work. I'm pretty sure you both should be, though."

"I called Sara, you're covered. Richard called Brad, he's covered. I called Peter, I'm covered. I think it's time for the wild monkey sex."

"Oh. Okay."

This time they all laughed, and it actually sounded genuine.

Chapter Sixteen

ഇ

Richard didn't know for sure if the next couple of hours qualified exactly as wild monkey sex, but neither could he bring himself to care. They made love and not to be too much of a dork, but he was pretty sure that they'd made a family. Of course, he hadn't exactly proved to be the most aware of what Caleb and Taryn were thinking when it came to the permanence of their relationship. Hell, he hadn't even been completely honest with himself in the beginning. But today had definitely felt right and good and real. And permanent.

Caleb led credence to his suspicions that they had all felt the same by suggesting they get dressed and go to *Roisin Dubh* to see who was playing and have dinner and drinks with his brother and sister-in-law. It was the first time he'd invited them there, the first time that he and Taryn would be going to the bar since meeting Caleb.

Caleb dropped him off at home with a promise to bring his things by. The freedom to move between their houses that he had enjoyed until today was suddenly irritating. It felt like more of a nuisance than a wealth of choices. He didn't want to figure out whose house had the leftovers, or the food that needed to be cooked, or the most laundry piled up or whatever. He didn't want to worry about overstepping his bounds at Caleb's or annoying himself by forgetting something he wanted at the wrong house. He wanted...simple. A home. A place they could make theirs, all of theirs.

The sound of the door opening nudged him from his musings and he stepped into the hallway, adjusting his belt. Hard, familiar hands grabbed him and pulled him in for a kiss, which he melted into. When Caleb stepped back he was breathing hard.

"You look hot," Caleb told him, presumably as explanation for the attack.

Richard frowned. He hadn't done anything special, just put on the jeans he knew Caleb liked and the shirt he knew Taryn liked.

He looked up to respond but it got stuck in his throat when he saw Caleb. The black jeans were tight in all the right places. The t-shirt was practically molded to his chest and the motorcycle boots lent an air of danger that had Richard wondering if Caleb knew how to ride one. Maybe they could…

Caleb snapped his fingers in front of his face and Richard blinked at him. Chuckling, Caleb just took his arm and dragged him out of the house, pausing while he activated the alarm. They arrived at Taryn's house about an hour after they'd left her. When she opened the door, however, it was a completely different Taryn.

She was wearing jeans, of course. She hardly ever wore anything other than jeans. But these must have been new, because he was sure he would remember her looking…like that. The tank top was one he had seen before but only managed to convince her to wear once. The muted green brought out the gold in her brown eyes, the top was cut low for her, enough to show the most enticing hint of her cleavage. It crossed over her breasts and wrapped around her middle, tying off on one side. The hem just met her jeans, so hints of skin peeked through as she moved, her reason for not wearing the top often.

"Amazing," was all that he could manage to say. His eyes made it up to her face, finally, and he saw that she was chewing on her lip just as Caleb reached over and tugged it out from beneath her teeth. She gave him a wry smile and closed the door behind her.

It was almost dinnertime when they got to the bar. Caleb led them to a table already occupied by a woman Richard recognized as Lisa.

"Lisa, you remember Taryn and Richard? This is my sister-in-law Lisa and here comes my brother Sean." They all shook hands and Lisa invited them to join her.

"We're expecting a big crowd tonight, I hope you're planning on staying awhile."

"I guess that depends on how well you feed us," Caleb answered with a smile as they all took seats.

"I heard there was some trouble out at your house this morning," Sean said, motioning a waiter over.

"Word travels fast," was Caleb's wry response. They all ordered drinks and Sean asked the waiter to bring menus. "It wasn't a big deal, the cops handled it. Hopefully that should be the end of the drama." He quickly sketched the situation.

"That's awful." Lisa's turned compassionate eyes on Richard. "For you to have to deal with this nonsense on top of the pain of losing your patient like that, I'm so sorry."

"I'm worried about the boy's mother, Elsie. This is not going to be easy for her." The waiter reappeared with drinks and menus. The Blacks waited while Richard and Taryn scanned the menu. It offered a standard collection of bar foods and Richard decided on one of his rarely permitted indulgences. He put the menu down and found Taryn watching him.

"Grilled cheese sandwich?" she asked.

"You know me too well." He grinned at her and watched while she made her own order. He'd hated seeing her so hurt this morning, hated that he was the cause, no matter how indirectly. He knew it was too much to hope that her issue was totally resolved now, but he felt confident that she had made some strong headway. Already she looked more comfortable around Caleb's family than he would have guessed she would be. He could tell it was partly forced, but once they began eating and drinking, he was sure she would relax.

A glance at Caleb found the other man watching him, not Taryn as he would have expected. He quirked an eyebrow in question.

"Grilled cheese?"

"What? I like cheese."

"Grilled cheese is for people who can't cook, and you can definitely cook."

"No, it's for people who like ooey, gooey yumminess."

Sean laughed and Lisa smacked Caleb on the shoulder. "Leave him alone, he can eat whatever he wants in our bar." She turned to Richard. "Have you guys noticed that a lot of your lives revolve around food and drink? Your family's restaurant, which I like very much, by the way, Grounded and here?"

Richard opened his mouth to make an automatic response, then realized that she was right. "Wow, no. I hadn't realized that before."

"Maybe we should start going to a gym," Taryn suggested.

"Hell," Caleb agreed, "we should probably invest in one."

"Or start buying some equipment, at the very least. We need a place with a basement so we can make our own gym. Then we can work out naked." As soon as the words left his mouth Richard remembered that there were other people at the table.

Sean and Lisa just laughed. "We got a treadmill after Katherine was born and we both had a fair amount of baby weight to work off," Sean told them. "Eventually we added a weight bench. I definitely preferred that to Lisa hanging out in a gym full of guys panting after her."

"I didn't mind that part. It was the bimbos who kept asking you to spot for them that annoyed me," Lisa reminded him archly.

Their food arrived just as a band started tuning up on the small stage. "These guys are good," Lisa assured them. "We've had them before and they always get people dancing."

Richard bit into his grilled cheese sandwich and managed to keep from moaning. He saw Caleb laughing at him silently, so he grinned and offered it up. Caleb met his eyes as he leaned in and took a big bite, licking his lips clean of cheese while he chewed.

Taryn cleared her throat and took a large sip of her beer, smiling behind the glass. Sean was studying his plate and Lisa was watching them, fascinated. Richard remembered that Caleb's family had rarely seen him with a girlfriend, and never with a boyfriend. He felt the heat crawling up his face.

"Katherine still enjoying school?" Caleb asked, breaking the quiet.

Lisa launched into a long narrative about her five-year-old's first month at school. Her pride was unmistakable and her pleasure very attractive. After a few minutes she wound down and flushed. "Sorry, I didn't mean to go on like that."

"You weren't," Taryn reassured her. "It must be tough for you, your baby out of the house most of the day now."

"Wellll…" Lisa drawled, glancing at her husband. She rested her hand on her flat stomach. "That won't be the case for too much longer."

They all congratulated Sean and Lisa until the couple rose. "It's time to call Katie and wish her a good night. We'll be right back," Sean told them. "You guys will stay awhile longer?"

"I think we're ready for another round of drinks, actually." Caleb stood and helped Sean take their plates to the kitchen, stopping at the bar on his way back to order fresh drinks for them.

Richard took Taryn's hand. "How're you doing, sweetie?"

"They're good people. I was a little worried, but I like them. I think Sean's a little weirded out, but as long as you don't start kissing each other in front of him, at least for a little while, he'll probably mellow."

Richard nodded, agreeing. Caleb returned with their drinks and a soda for himself. "Katherine spends Thursday dinners with Lisa's parents so that they can watch over the bar together. They split up the other nights between them and a manager. The baby is good news. They've actually been trying for a couple of years and were starting to get worried."

"That is good news," Taryn said. She cocked her head and eyed them both. "We should talk about that, you know."

"If we're all ready to acknowledge that there's a future for us. All of us," Caleb agreed. "We should talk about that, and a lot more."

Sean and Lisa returned to the table and they turned the conversation to the college football team's chances for the season. The band began to pick things up a bit as more people finished their meals. When Taryn started fidgeting in her chair, Richard asked her to dance. She hopped up immediately, earning a laugh from both Richard and Caleb.

Leading her to the dance area, Richard felt like the eyes of everyone at their table were on them. He spun Taryn around and used the opportunity to look back, but Sean and Lisa were talking to a waiter, leaving only Caleb watching them. The heat and promise in his smile nearly made Richard falter in his steps.

"Hey," Taryn laughed, punching him lightly in the shoulder. "You're supposed to be watching me, not Studly."

Snickering at that, Richard focused his attention appropriately. "I dare you to call him that to his face."

Her haughty look took up the challenge. "You think I won't?"

With a laugh, he swept her into his arms and swung her around.

"I love you," he told her, placing her gently on her feet.

"I know," she sighed, tossing her hair back dramatically. "I'm irresistible."

"At least to some," he agreed, twirling her again.

"So long as it's the right 'some', I'm good with it."

The band changed to a slow song and he brought her in close.

"We should drive up to the city one of these nights, go to a gay bar so we can all dance together," Taryn murmured, her head a sweet weight on his shoulder, her hands lightly caressing his back.

"That would be nice. We could do a long weekend, take a mini-vacation."

"Yeah. Ricky, do you think this is all too fast? Talking love and vacations, houses and babies?"

"I do think it's fast, but I don't think it's too fast. I think it's one of those 'you'll know it when you find it' things. This is so far and away different than what I've experienced before that I have almost no doubts."

"Almost?"

Richard paused, hoping he could find the right words. "The thing with Paul Jones, even though it was annoying and scary, it didn't really affect us, you know? But what if we all move in together and people freak? My patients, your customers, Caleb's clients? They have a direct impact on our lives. I guess I just wonder how we'll handle that."

The song ended and Taryn pulled back, looking at him.

"We should talk about that, too. Like Caleb said, there's a lot we should talk about." She took his hand and led him back to the table.

By the time they left, Richard was pleased to see that Taryn seemed to be enjoying Caleb's family as much as he was. They were both a little bit buzzed, which reminded them all of that first night as they exited the bar.

"We could have taken a taxi home again, Caleb. You didn't have to stop at one drink." Taryn took Caleb's hand and twirled herself around.

"I was keeping Lisa company. Did you put your hand on Sean's ass when you two were dancing?"

"Well, sure and I did, Studly," she answered with an affected Irish accent. "And a fine ass it 'tis."

"Richard managed to keep his hands off Lisa's ass," Caleb pointed out, giving her a quizzical look at the nickname.

"Well," she answered, thankfully dropping the brogue, "in my ever-so-humble opinion, Lisa's ass has nothing on Sean's. And Sean's has nothing on either of yours. Either. Too. Whatever."

They loaded into the car and drove to Richard's house. He took the time now that he hadn't during his brief stop earlier, to water the plants and open some windows. It was amazing what a few days away could do to an empty house.

By the time he made it to the bedroom, Caleb was propped up against the headboard with Taryn draped across his lap, sound asleep. Caleb was stroking her hair but his eyes were on Richard.

Richard unbuttoned his shirt. "She had a long day."

"We all did. Did you talk to Laura earlier?" His voice was even but his eyes were on Richard's hands as they unzipped his pants.

"Yes, he was spouting something about being God's tool, so they're sure now he's the one who painted the house and knifed the tires. They're still working on the murder charge. They're going to do a psych evaluation on the guy."

Caleb nodded. "I expected as much from the way he was behaving. Do you think it was an act?"

"No, it felt genuine to me. I think I'll call Mrs. Jones tomorrow, see how she's doing. I haven't spoken to her since the funeral." He shucked his underwear and headed into the bathroom. When he came back into the room Caleb was gently moving Taryn to the side so that he could move down on the bed. Richard turned out the light and slid in next to Caleb.

"Tired?" Caleb asked him.

"Not too tired. Kiss me."

"Getting kind of demanding, aren't you?" Caleb asked, his voice low and gravelly.

"I have my days."

Caleb swooped in and halted further conversation with a hard kiss. He tasted of a hint of beer and he felt like heaven. Richard relaxed as Caleb's weight pressed into him, the hard length of cock pressing into his leg.

The kisses changed, going from hard to soft, fast to slow, until Richard was chasing Caleb, trying to bring him back. Caleb held himself just out of reach and Richard moaned in denial.

"Tell me what you want." Caleb's whisper was so quiet Richard almost didn't hear him over the blood rushing through his head.

"You." He reached up, intending to pull Caleb's head back down, but the other man took his wrists firmly in hand and held them above his head.

"Are you done fighting this then?" His voice was serious and Richard fought to understand.

"What?"

"This. Us. Are you ours? Are you done hiding?"

"Yes, Caleb. No more hiding. All yours." He was panting and working hard not to struggle in Caleb's grasp. Didn't he know? Didn't they both know that he was theirs and he wasn't letting them go either?

"I want you, I want you both. I want a home, for all of us."

"That's good, because I'm not letting you go. Now tell me, what do you want me to do?" Caleb sat up a bit so that his knees pressed against Richard's sides, holding him still.

Richard couldn't quite get his brain to function. "I want you." He lifted his head again, trying to reach those firm lips, but Caleb brought one hand down to bracket his throat, keeping Richard's head still while he rained kisses along his cheek, suckled his earlobe. Richard could only face forward, trying to concentrate on what Caleb had asked him.

"I want you inside of me. I want you to kiss me again."

"Hold onto the headboard. Don't let go." Caleb released his wrists and his throat and retrieved a condom and lube from the bedside drawer.

Kneeling up over him, Caleb looked dark and dangerous and oh-so sexy. Richard couldn't believe that this man belonged to him. In hardly more than a month, he knew that to be true. Caleb was his, and Taryn's. Taryn was his, and Caleb's. And he. He belonged to both of them, and nothing had ever made him feel so wonderful.

He wanted to let go so that he could help Caleb with the condom, but he tightened his grip on the headboard. Caleb took his time rolling the condom on, then rubbed himself absently while watching Richard.

"Please, Caleb."

As he moved down Richard's body, Caleb leaned in and left a wet trail of kisses in his wake. Finally Caleb squirted lube onto his fingers but instead of putting them inside he used his hand to squeeze Richard's cock, making it even harder. He rubbed his thumb over the head then brought his other hand up to lift and tug on his balls.

Richard gasped in pleasure. Sweat coated his whole body and he ached to feel Caleb's weight on him again. "Caleb."

The hand on his shaft tightened further but the other hand returned to the lube. Richard nearly rejoiced when slick fingers tickled his hole. He bucked his hips as much as he could into the hand holding him, then came down on the fingers seeking entrance. Two fingers impaled him and he bit off a moan. Twisting and turning, the fingers opened him up, but he needed more. "Caleb," he whispered again, begging.

Caleb released his cock and surged up his body, mouth landing on mouth, chest hard against chest. Richard opened for him, tongue and cock filling him in one swift surge. He cried out, though it was mostly muffled as he eagerly matched Caleb's dueling tongue. He bent his legs, fighting for leverage, meeting Caleb's thrusts. The angle made the friction of Caleb's hard abdomen against his straining dick send him over the edge. He clamped his muscles hard and Caleb came, collapsing fully against him.

Richard was just starting to think he should clean up when he heard Taryn stretch next to them. He and Caleb both turned to look at her. Taryn's eyes were half closed, the sheet kicked away, her hand between her legs, her smile somehow both sweet and naughty. "Pretty," she whispered, then let her eyes close fully.

Caleb got up to fetch washcloths. Richard took the opportunity to pull Taryn into him. She came willingly, pillowing her head on his shoulder. When Caleb lay down at his side, he wrapped his long arm around both of them. Richard was almost asleep when Taryn shifted.

"I've been thinking." Her voice was a drowsy murmur. Richard wasn't convinced she was entirely awake.

"Hmmm?" Caleb asked.

"I don't want to get married." She said it offhand, but Richard opened his eyes and saw Caleb prop up on his elbow.

"Now?" Richard asked.

"Ever. I mean, it's silly, don't you think?"

"Well—" Caleb's response was cut off as sleeping Taryn apparently wasn't finished.

"It's not like any of us go to church, so I don't really care about the whole saying I love you in front of a priest thing. And I don't need the government to tell me we're family."

"How ab—" This time it was Richard who tried to speak, unsuccessfully.

"Seriously, whose business is it that we're in love and want to be together forever? Our families will certainly get the point when we move in together and make a life together and have babies and stuff."

There was silence as both Richard and Caleb waited to see if more was coming. More came in the form of a small snore.

"Taryn?" Caleb's voice was much more tentative than Richard had ever heard before.

No response.

"I think she's still asleep," Richard murmured.

"I think you're right. Do you suppose she'll remember any of this in the morning?"

"No clue. Do you agree with what she said?"

"I couldn't care less who she wants to formalize the commitment with as long as she makes the commitment." Caleb was starting to sound sleepy.

"I think the big test will be giving up her apartment."

"You're right. What about you? You want the church wedding and all the trappings?"

"Whatever. As long as I have you both." Richard yawned and closed his eyes.

"Good answer."

Chapter Seventeen
Two months later

ഔ

Caleb paused in the act of climbing into the back of the moving truck to watch Taryn and Richard negotiate the walkway while sharing the load of a coffee table. They were arguing good-naturedly about the hassles of moving.

"We would have been moved in by now if you hadn't insisted on completely remodeling the kitchen," Taryn grumbled.

"I wouldn't have insisted on that if you didn't insist on eating," Richard responded. "Besides, we still would have had to do all this."

A nudge on his shoulder had Caleb glancing away from Taryn's ass to see his brother watching him. "I knew there were downsides to having two lovers. Do they squabble like that a lot?"

Caleb managed to keep a straight face. "Only out of bed. But don't get me wrong, it's a lot of work keeping two people satisfied. One likes coffee, one likes Coke. One likes showers, one likes baths. One wants a new stove, one wants a pool."

"Uh-huh. And the upsides?"

"Oh brother. The upsides are nearly limitless. There's always someone to enjoy a meal with, to bathe with, to cook with, to swim naked with. To sit on the couch and watch a movie with or to jog with. Plus, a whole extra set of hands." He glanced back at the couple. "You know, to help on moving day."

"Riiiight," Sean drawled.

"And of course, when you just want to be alone, there's someone else around they can go bug."

"One of the reasons," Sean agreed, pulling a dining room chair out of the truck, "that we wanted a second kid."

Caleb laughed and followed him into the house with a second chair. They found Richard and Taryn sprawled on the sofa, feet on the coffee table they had just been carrying. Caleb thought he might join them but then Mama came in from the kitchen and gave them the evil eye before spotting Caleb and Sean. She gave them a huge grin and went back to the kitchen. Somehow, and he really didn't know how but wasn't going to complain, Mama had become his biggest fan.

Taryn hopped up and went to help Emma with the large armful of clothes that she was trying to negotiate down the hall. Richard's brother gave him a hand up and they went back to the truck for another load.

Four hours later everything was moved in and all of their friends and family had left. They were in the Jacuzzi, exhausted.

"Please tell me we never have to do that again," Taryn said. She moved so that a jet was pulsing at her back and groaned.

"We never have to do that again," Caleb confirmed, pulling her into his lap so that he could massage her shoulders.

"Unless we have so many kids we need a bigger house," Richard added.

"I think we were all clear that three kids would be plenty, and that's perfect for this house," Taryn reminded him. "Besides, I like an equal parent-to-kid ratio. Means we have a fighting chance."

"Well, now that we have the house, think we should work on filling it up?" Richard asked.

"Not until it's perfect, which for you may mean never. I can't believe how many stores we had to go to just to pick out a couch." Taryn laid her head back against Caleb's shoulder so he stopped massaging and wrapped his hands around her.

"True, but it looks great in that room. And it's comfy as hell," Caleb said.

"Yeah."

"That reminds me of something I wanted to ask you guys," Richard said.

"Does it involve furniture shopping?" Taryn asked.

"No, jewelry shopping."

That peaked Taryn's interest and she turned her head to study Richard.

"Jewelry is good."

"I understand," Richard said slowly, "your position on marriage, the ceremony and everything. But I thought it might be nice if we went and got some rings. All three of us."

Caleb's arms tightened around Taryn.

"Oh," she said. "Yeah, that sounds good. I like that plan."

They stayed silent for a time, enjoying the hot, bubbly water in the cool night air.

"Richard. Caleb."

"Taryn."

"I'm glad we're here."

Caleb stood up, holding Taryn until she set her feet down. "Let's go inside."

After drying off, they made their way to the master bedroom, turning off lights and closing windows. The house that had belonged to his parents was now theirs, all of theirs. They each owned a third and had spent the last three weeks co-managing the renovations and choosing the furniture and appliances. Lisa's family's construction company had done the work, quickly and cheaply. This complete acceptance by not only his and Richard's families but Lisa's as well had meant a great deal to all three of them.

They made it into the bedroom and Taryn took their wet towels to the bathroom while Richard went to adjust the heater. Caleb checked around and found the box labeled M. Bedroom 3. Unlike some of the boxes, this one had been taped shut so he looked around until he found something he could slice through the tape with. Finally spotting scissors on top of another unopened box, he made quick work of it and found the condoms and lube right where they should be. He pulled them out and turned around.

Candles were set out on the surfaces that were not yet too cluttered and Richard was lighting them. Caleb realized Taryn must have arranged them after her shower, while he and Richard were getting dinner ready. Deciding the candles were a good start, Caleb went to the stereo that Laura had helped her brother set up and checked the CD. It was one of Richard's favorite jazz discs, so he left it in and turned it on low.

From the different parts of the room, they came together slowly. Arms slid around waists and shoulders, mouths touched, bodies swayed. It was all so…right.

"Taryn," Caleb murmured, just loud enough to get her attention. He knew that she would hear not just the words but the soft command. She turned her eyes to him, waiting, always ready.

"Yes, Caleb."

"Kiss Richard."

Her smile was soft and sweet and she wasted no time following his order. Richard stayed still, letting her reach up for him, letting her pull him to her, willingly following her lead and Caleb's instructions. He watched them kiss, watched Richard's arms twitch as they automatically moved to encircle his lover, but stayed at his side because he had not yet been told he could move.

Stepping behind him, Caleb rested his hands on Richard's shoulders and leaned in to lick the smooth skin between his shoulder blades. Clean but sweaty in a very good way. Caleb moved his hands down muscled arms until they covered Richard's. Lacing their fingers together, he guided Richard's hands to Taryn's waist, up the curve to her rib cage and in to her breasts. They explored there, together, until Taryn was panting, her nipples hard points jabbing at Richard's palms, begging to be suckled.

"Taryn, get on the bed." Caleb heard the roughness in his voice, felt Richard shiver against him, saw Taryn squeeze her legs closed in reaction.

Backing away from them, Taryn reached behind her to find the bed then slowly scooted onto it, never looking away. When she was in the center, knees bent and splayed wide so they could see her wetness calling to them, she propped herself on her elbows and waited.

Arms wrapped around Richard, Caleb leaned close into his ear and whispered so that Taryn couldn't hear. "Breasts, then pussy. Tongue only." Richard nodded and they advanced.

Climbing up on either side of her, they went straight to her straining nipples, sucking them in hard and fast. Taryn cried out and Caleb heard Richard release his prize with a pop before returning for more. Caleb lashed the nub with his tongue then nibbled all around it. He ran into Richard in the valley between her breasts and paused to kiss the man he loved so much. When they separated he jerked his head south and they moved down her body as one, kissing and licking a path to where she wanted them most.

Caleb got off the bed and knelt at the edge, using Taryn's ankles to drag her closer. Richard lay down next to her, one arm draped over her abdomen as he bent to kiss her waiting clit, Caleb holding her folds open to give him easy access. Taryn bucked when Richard sucked the bundle of nerves into his mouth. Caleb left Richard to his task and moved down, breathing heavily on her curls to remind her that there was more to come.

Delicately, Caleb swirled his tongue through the folds, circled her opening but didn't go in. He pulled back and watched as her interior muscles squeezed her opening, begging to be penetrated. He couldn't resist such an invitation and filled her as much as he could with his tongue. Jerking, she caused him to bump heads with Richard, which made him chuckle. She gasped at the sensation this caused and he could tell she was close.

Again, he drew back, blowing on her wet folds, watching Richard suck her clit. He waited until she was clearly struggling to hold back her release.

"Mmm, so good, baby, I love the way you taste."

Richard stopped, licking his lips and looking longingly at her pussy. Caleb laughed and kissed him, giving him her taste that way. Richard groaned and fed freely, while they listened to Taryn's breathing even out. Pulling back, Caleb led Richard on a kissing journey back up her body, until he reached her neck. Her breathing had picked up again by the time he found the sweet spot behind her ear. Satisfied, he sat up, Richard following his lead, smiling when Taryn whimpered.

Offering Taryn a hand, Caleb pulled her to her feet, then sat on the edge of the bed. He rested one foot on the frame of the bed, leaving plenty of room in front of himself.

"Taryn, kneel here." He pointed to the space in front of him, slightly to the left of center. She dropped to her knees, her eyes glued to his cock.

"Richard, kneel behind her, and to the side here," he pointed. There was just enough space that Richard could kneel partly behind and partly to the side of Taryn, his face over her shoulder.

"Suck me, Taryn. Richard, you can use your hands and mouth, but don't let her come."

Taryn's hot mouth engulfed the head of his cock, and he had to clench his teeth not to shout. He brushed the drying hair back from her face so he could see himself filling her small

193

mouth. She used her hands to caress his shaft, startling when Richard's tongue found her ear as his fingers found her wet folds.

Caleb watched, entranced, as one of Richard's hands worked her pussy and the other made its way down her arm to join her smaller hand wrapped around his dick. This time he did groan as the larger hand squeezed the smaller hand tight around his hard length. Richard kissed down her jaw, which was opened wide around its burden. Caleb groaned again as Taryn pulled free to kiss Richard, then offered Richard his dick like it was an ice-cream cone.

Richard must have done something to Taryn that Caleb couldn't see because she squeezed her eyes shut, breathing deeply to stave off her release. Richard took the opportunity to lick Caleb around Taryn's fingers before sucking the head in.

"Up." Caleb had to clear his throat and try again to get the word to come out as more than a croak. "Up."

They both gave him one last lick before helping each other to their feet. Caleb grabbed a condom and handed it to Richard. Once it was on he grabbed the man by the back of the neck and kissed him, hard. Not releasing his mouth or his neck, he backed Richard up until he had him where he wanted him. Finally, he pulled back.

"Taryn, get the plugs from the box and lube one up." He went back to kissing while Taryn rummaged through the box. He heard her giggling and knew without a doubt that she was remembering the morning she'd opened the dishwasher and screamed at finding the two silicone toys inside, freshly cleaned. Still kissing, he turned Richard around and presented his backside to Taryn.

To help, he palmed the taut ass cheeks and pulled them apart. Richard moaned as Taryn pushed the plug inside. Caleb turned him around again and presented his own backside to Taryn. "I'll take the other one." Richard broke the kiss to glance at Taryn but Caleb bit him on the chin and pulled him in for more.

He felt Taryn's tentative touch, then Richard's hands as they gave her the same help he had. The plug went in easily and he clenched his muscles when it was seated fully. Taryn took the opportunity to nip his buttock then lick the spot, sending electricity through his whole body. His dick jerked against Richard's and they both moaned. Pulling back, he let Richard go.

Taking Taryn's hand, he pulled her up beside him and gestured that she should follow him. While his hand went down to find Richard's cock, his mouth went to the man's nipple. Together they gave him the same treatment Taryn had received.

Caleb pulled back and put his hands at Taryn's hips. He lifted her up and she wrapped her legs around Richard's waist. Richard's hands came up to hold her to him and Caleb let go. He kissed Taryn's shoulder and palmed Richard's cock, bringing it to her entrance. She moaned and slid down, Richard helping her control the descent. When she was seated, they paused, waiting for his instructions. He could see the excitement in both of their faces.

The truth was, they could have done this weeks ago, but it had come to mean more than a physical act to Taryn, and Caleb knew that. It had become more than fantasy, something of a symbol of their relationship, the three of them together. Now, in their new house, it was time.

He got another condom, put it on, then lubed his fingers liberally. Richard leaned back against the wall for support and used his hands to open her wide. Caleb brought one finger to her puckered hole and eased it in. She remained perfectly still, resting her head on Richard's shoulder. He added another finger and she squirmed against him. With his other hand he reached around and plucked at Richard's balls then moved to Taryn's clit.

Shit, they were so hot. How could he ever get enough of them? After Taryn's sleepy talk about marriage, he and Richard had privately agreed to wait until she brought it up again on her own. When she'd finally broached the subject of the three of them moving in together, he and Richard practically had her signing mortgage papers before the sentence was all the way out of her mouth.

He looked at them, watched them while he lubed his cock, stroking himself, knowing he had never been as happy as he would be in the morning, waking up in their bed, in their house, with the knowledge that it was only the first of many mornings.

Ready, he brought his cock to her hole and eased in slowly. She stiffened at first at the unaccustomed width, then bore down on him. He could feel Richard through her sheath, as he moved slowly inside.

"Caleb," Richard groaned as he slid past.

"Caleb," Taryn moaned as he seated himself fully.

They were still as the perfection of the moment hit them. Finally, Caleb could stand it no more.

"Move as you want," he whispered, pulling out. "Come when you want," he added as Richard pulled out. He thrust in, then withdrew, Richard working in counterpoint. Every time he was inside her, Taryn clenched around him and he squeezed his own muscles around the plug, adding to the exquisite pleasure.

They didn't last long. Taryn came first, loud and long as they continued to move within her. Caleb held back, determined to send Richard over. He reached around but didn't have time to do anything before Richard climaxed with a shout. Caleb could hold back no longer and spilled himself into Taryn.

Pressing them both against the wall, he leaned over Taryn's shoulder and kissed Richard softly, gently, before helping Taryn down. He turned her around and kissed her just as gently. Perfect, they were both so perfect.

"I love you," Caleb told them both, again, always.

They responded in unison, in a way that he hoped would never fail to make his heart squeeze, as it did now.

"Yes, Caleb.

Also by KB Alan

ဆ

eBooks:
Alpha Turned
Bound by Sunlight
Perfect Formation

About the Author

ജ

KB Alan lives the single life in Southern California. She acknowledges that she should probably turn off the computer and leave the house once in a while in order to find her own happily ever after, but for now she's content to delude herself with the theory that Mr. Right is bound to come knocking on her door through no real effort on her own. Please refrain from pointing out the many flaws in this system. Other comments, however, are happily received through her email or website.

KB Alan welcomes comments from readers. You can find her website and email address on her author bio page at www.ellorascave.com.

Tell Us What You Think

We appreciate hearing reader opinions about our books. You can email us at Comments@EllorasCave.com.

Why an electronic book?

We live in the Information Age — an exciting time in the history of human civilization, in which technology rules supreme and continues to progress in leaps and bounds every minute of every day. For a multitude of reasons, more and more avid literary fans are opting to purchase e-books instead of paper books. The question from those not yet initiated into the world of electronic reading is simply: *Why?*

1. *Price.* An electronic title at Ellora's Cave Publishing and Cerridwen Press runs anywhere from 40% to 75% less than the cover price of the exact same title in paperback format. Why? Basic mathematics and cost. It is less expensive to publish an e-book (no paper and printing, no warehousing and shipping) than it is to publish a paperback, so the savings are passed along to the consumer.

2. *Space.* Running out of room in your house for your books? That is one worry you will never have with electronic books. For a low one-time cost, you can purchase a handheld device specifically designed for e-reading. Many e-readers have large, convenient screens for viewing. Better yet, hundreds of titles can be stored within your new library — on a single microchip. There are a variety of e-readers from different manufacturers. You can also read e-books on your PC or laptop computer. (Please note that Ellora's Cave does not endorse any specific brands.

You can check our websites at www.ellorascave.com or www.cerridwenpress.com for information we make available to new consumers.)

3. *Mobility.* Because your new e-library consists of only a microchip within a small, easily transportable e-reader, your entire cache of books can be taken with you wherever you go.

4. *Personal Viewing Preferences.* Are the words you are currently reading too small? Too large? Too... ANNOYING? Paperback books cannot be modified according to personal preferences, but e-books can.

5. *Instant Gratification.* Is it the middle of the night and all the bookstores near you are closed? Are you tired of waiting days, sometimes weeks, for bookstores to ship the novels you bought? Ellora's Cave Publishing sells instantaneous downloads twenty-four hours a day, seven days a week, every day of the year. Our webstore is never closed. Our e-book delivery system is 100% automated, meaning your order is filled as soon as you pay for it.

Those are a few of the top reasons why electronic books are replacing paperbacks for many avid readers.

As always, Ellora's Cave and Cerridwen Press welcome your questions and comments. We invite you to email us at Comments@ellorascave.com or write to us directly at Ellora's Cave Publishing Inc., 1056 Home Avenue, Akron, OH 44310-3502.

COMING TO A BOOKSTORE NEAR YOU!

ELLORA'S CAVE

Bestselling Authors Tour

ELLORA'S CAVE
Romanticon

Annual convention
for women who
refuse to behave

COLUMBUS DAY WEEKEND

8709809R0

Made in the USA
Lexington, KY
24 February 2011